2013 — 2014 ANTHOLOGY

NEIGHBORHOOD GUILD CREATIVE WRITERS GROUP

EDITED BY JANE MAXSON

COMPILED BY

MYRINA CARDELLA-MARENGHI
AND
LINDA LANGLOIS

PHOTOGRAPHY BY C. DAVIS FOGG

To Stephanie ~
Enjoy Cheryl

TABLE OF CONTENTS

DEDICATED

TO

PATRICIA L. FRÖHLICH

The serendipity of The Neighborhood Guild Thursday Writers is the people you meet who belong to the writers: their friends, families and their special people. And, sometimes, these special people become special to you as well.

So it was with Patricia, Professor Reinhard Fröhlich's wife. The Emerald Isle itself shone through her laughing Irish eyes. She'd open her mouth and all of Dublin was in her voice.

The Irish Blessing is on her *Goodbye* card from Avery-Storti. She left us on March 1st, sixteen days shy of her 81st birthday.

We, The Neighborhood Guild Thursday Writers, wish to pay special tribute to her.

To this end, we dedicate this 2014 Anthology to a special lass if ever there was one.

######

INTRODUCTION
By Linda Langlois

AN OPEN LETTER TO THE NEIGHBORHOOD GUILD CREATIVE WRITERS...
By Linda Langlois

Dear Thursday Folks:

The prompt was *Silence.*
The response crossed countries, generations and time.

With your words, I stood beside you in Notre Dame, where you were drawn from the streets of Paris by Vivaldi's organ concert, his music majestically clamoring, slamming against the rafters till the sound was almost unbearable, and in an instant—*silence*—total absolute *silence*, your heartbeat—the only sound.

A woman, whose sense of sound is not her first language, stands in a kitchen doorway feeling the sun warm upon her face. She sees the school bus rounding the corner, sees the children laughing, the whole scene caught as in a silent movie. She's remembering the summer, lying in total silence on warm sand, at peace with her inner world.

Upstairs, in an alcove bedroom of teddy bears and bunny rabbit wallpaper, the silence turns beneath the drone of a mother's vacuum. While nothing seems amiss among her daily chores, the mother's antenna vibrates. Investigation finds her four-year-old boys out on the roof, two stories above a concrete sidewalk.

A woman lies awake in a silent night where *"wind rustles the leaves, waves splash rhythmically on the shore deer munch on shrubbery under her window and a tiny mouse scrabbles, searching for crumbs under the kitchen sink."* At 3 am, *"a time when the sounds of silence are magnified,"* she wonders, is *silence* ever silent?

Noise is everywhere: loud music on the street, in grocery stores and in restaurants, not always your favorite piece ... One must plan a time and place for silence.

In a year of change and great loss, people disappearing and new friends appearing, this prompt, *Silence,* most overwhelmed me with your responses. It seemed to resonate, somehow, the year this was.

To all of you, I dedicate *"The Case of the Missing Scriveners."* These are your stories taken from your writings and what you said along the way. You are all in this piece, your identities tucked inside your words.

Thank you for sharing all of yourselves with me,

Linda

Mary interviewed Monica after acting as her secretary for a period of several years. Mary is the daughter of Betty Cotter, who led our group for years and with whom we continue to have a close relationship. Mary is currently an entrant in the 2015 Miss Rhode Island contest.

Monica's Note: Mary A. Cotter became my "Secretary" when I was finally presented with a computer.

Why did I refuse to engage with my computer? Well, I seem to remember that I vowed never to touch a typewriter again and my computer seemed to bear a resemblance. So, my good fortune was to find Mary A. Cotter, daughter of Betty Cotter. Mary was young, computer savvy – and available.

Mary came every Friday and she typed out all my answers to the waiting worlds: my friends in New York City, Acapulco, Mexico, Israel and London, England.

Mary is a quiet, lovely young lady but when I read her "Interview with Monica Hickey—Bridal Extraordinaire," I knew she was Betty Cotter's daughter:

o o o o o o o o

MONICA HICKEY – Bridal Extraordinaire
By Mary A. Cotter
Sitting in her stylish living room in her new-found home of Wakefield, Monica Hickey talks about her very own bridal

department in New York, "The Bridal World of Monica Hickey," as if it is, in fact, a world away. Of course, as usual, she throws in her chimes of encouragement to join the fashion industry in between stories, claiming once again that if I "become a journalist, I'll have to travel to Africa and catch some horrible disease," chuckling at the absurdity in her charming British accent. Monica was, in her day, at the very center of the bridal industry and some may argue that she still is, still taking annual road trips to New York to rub elbows with some of her dearest friends on Fifth Avenue. Standing at about 4'11," Monica bustles through the two-story condo looking for her various notes on the happenings of that day.

Spontaneously, you're asking me something from a long time ago. When I was in London and I met the young couple, the Emanuel's, who were just out of design school, but they had a beautiful salon. So, I invited them to come to Henri Bendel to have a trunk show, because they did wedding dresses and I was in buying. They had a whole page in the New York Times, and then when they went back to London, Lady Diana invited them to do her entire wardrobe for her wedding.

And then, there was when Vera Wang was looking for a wedding dress and couldn't find one and she came to Saks and I saw her in the salon wandering around and I asked, "Can I help you?" And she said, "Yes," that she wanted someone to design the most beautiful wedding dress.

I had a German designer, who did very fancy and delicate wedding dresses. So, we both did sketches and designed a proposed wedding dress. It was a slim column of satin, the first strapless wedding dress created with Vera Wang. But she had beautiful beaded flowers. It wasn't just at the shoulders, those today (*motioning with her hands the strapless silhouette*) awful things.

She changed three times at the wedding. The dress she wore down the aisle, she didn't wear all night, which I think was a great idea. She took me to meet her father, a multi-millionaire (*eyebrows raised*), of Wang pharmaceuticals in China. This was years ago. When they offered me a contract, my husband, Peter, asked me, "*Do you want to be a bird in a gilded cage?*" And I said, "*No, not really.*" But I was a consultant, which was very nice. That took care of that.

Jill Krementz, who came from Rhode Island—they were the jewelry people. I don't think they have it now. Um, Jill Krementz wanted something very simple. She had a tea length, which I love and it was all antique lace. And she married Kurt Vonnegut. And they did not live happily every after, which is not guaranteed by anyone (*she said chidingly*). Right? Right. He was famous (*she paused*) in World War II when he was captured by the Germans and he went to Dresden. And that was the time when the British and the Americans bombed, flattened the most beautiful place in the world. And he came out of the cellar and survived. But their wedding was beautiful. Jill said, "My mother makes me nervous," so I sat with her in the car to the church. She's a very interesting woman. So that was it. Their wedding had the celebrities of the world, all these famous authors. Is that enough about them (*she asked.*) I mean it can't be all about me (*she said, laughing as I told her that it was, in fact, all about her.*)

I never wore a real wedding dress; I don't like them. I don't like, personally, to be on show and I just didn't like that. I wore a tea length, hand-crocheted, two-piece, and that was it, and beautiful shoes. I think it's what I did, but whatever the people want to do is fine with me and it paid off because I loved what I did.

It's like being an actress and you get a part to play, but you're still yourself inside. You're not for sale and that's why people came to Bergdorf's, Bendel's, everywhere, because they trusted me.

Monica swiftly herds me out of her home, promising to call me soon once she has more people to write to, laughing, saying she has no friends left. I assure her that she, in fact, has many.

######

HONEY

By Jane Maxson

"Mommy, look at me. I'm flying." My tiny four-year-old pumped her legs and soared forward and back on the swing, her brown pigtails bobbing.

"Don't go any higher, Honey," I cautioned, as I turned to check on baby Billy in his carriage. I tucked the blanket closer around him to keep out the cool April breeze. He was only three months new and easily chilled.

I turned back to tell Honey to power down and land. But she was no longer on the swing. "Honey," I called, "Come on. It's time to go home. Where are you? Are you hiding? There's no more time for games. We have to go. It's almost time for Daddy to come home."

She wasn't behind the rhododendron bushes that grew along the fence at the edge of the park, nor could I see her skipping down the walk toward the entrance.

"Come on, Sweetie, time to go home." I called, getting annoyed. Why had she chosen this time to disappear?

Pushing the carriage, I began trotting toward the park entrance. Where could she have gone? At the entrance, I looked up and down the sidewalk, but Honey was not in sight. She was very good about not crossing the road without holding my hand, but could she have ventured across?

Now, I was getting worried! There were stories on the news about children being kidnapped and sold, or horrible thought, molested. Old Sam Brown came shuffling up the street and I stopped him. "Mr. Brown, have you seen Honey?"

"Nope, why? Is she lost?"

"She was on the swing and suddenly she was gone."

"She's such a little tyke. She can't have gone far," he assured me and turned to continue on his way.

"What should I do? Go home and phone the police, or continue looking around the park?" I crossed over to the big Victorian house on the corner, climbed the porch steps and pulled the old-fashioned bell knob all the time keeping an eye on the carriage. The heavy oak door creaked open a crack and an elderly woman peered at me, said, "We don't want any," and slammed the door. I frantically pulled the knob again, but no one came.

Just then, my neighbor, Karen, walked around the corner.

"Karen," I called, running down the steps, "Will you help me look for Honey? She was on the swing. I turned my back to check on Billy and suddenly she was gone! I looked, but couldn't find her anywhere."

" I have my cell phone. Do you want me to call the police? They can do a more thorough search."

"Oh please call. I was trying to get the woman in that house to let me use her phone."

In a short time, a police car pulled up at the gate to the park and a very young looking policeman stepped out. "I'm Officer Ryan. You've lost a child?"

"Yes. She was on the swing one minute and the next she was gone. I can't figure out how she stopped swinging, got off and disappeared so quickly."

"I'll have a look around. She can't have gone too far," Ryan said. He walked into the park and began pacing methodically along the fence looking around and under the shrubbery. He stopped abruptly near a heavy clump of bushes.

"Hey," he called, "did you know there was a shed back here?"

"No. I had no idea. Is it open?"

"No, it's barred."

I raced across the grass, pushing the carriage over the uneven sod and called, "Honey! Honey, are you in there?" There was no answer.

"Shall I break it open?" Ryan asked.

"Go ahead. She could be in there and can't answer for some reason."

Officer Ryan removed the two-by-four that held the door shut and pushed it open. I rushed past him and saw Honey huddled in a corner, mouth taped and hands and ankles tied.

Karen was behind me and warned, "Let me take her picture with my phone before you untie her."

I waited impatiently as the picture was taken, then rushed to my daughter who was crying softly. Carefully removing the tape from her mouth I untied her bonds, picked her up and hugged her tight, whispering, "Oh Honey, what happened?"

"Mommy," she sobbed, "Two big boys pulled me off the swing put tape on my mouth and carried me here. They tied me up and told me to stay here and be quiet until they came back."

"You take your children home, Mrs. Perry, and I'll wait here for the boys to come back," Officer Ryan instructed.

We headed off with Karen pushing the carriage while I carried Honey home to safety.

April, 2014

######

SATURDAY

By Jane Maxson

It's Saturday again

But I wonder when

I lived through

The other days?

Where was I on Monday?

And Friday is a blur

Now Saturday has come again

Another week has gone

And here I am

Wondering

Pondering

What happened to those other days?

Why are there so many

Saturdays?

March, 2014

######

LETTER TO MY PARENTS

By Jane Maxson

Dear Mom and Dad,

I never really thanked you for the happy secure life you gave me. So let me say it now. It's been almost fifty years since you left and I think of you often. I think of you when I look at my children, your grandchildren. You would be proud of the adults they have become and thrilled to see their children, your great grandchildren, all grown now.

Mom, thank you for always wanting the best for me. You went to work during the war and proudly became more than just a secretary. You finished your employment as a cost estimator with enough salary to help pay for my college expenses and make sure I had an appropriate wardrobe for my college years. You were the ambitious one who thought I should attend UConn, not just Willimantic Teachers' College. I was happy to be going to college when most of my high school friends were going to work. Girls who were in college prep courses with me were expected to work in their fathers' stores, or clerk in the local factories.

Mom, you were the one who preached, "Marry one of your own kind." and found flaws in the boys I dated. "He's never going to be more than a carpenter," or, "You'll never be happy with him, he's too restless." But when I made up my mind on the guy I wanted to marry, you finally accepted him, after pointing out what you considered his flaws. After I married, you helped by providing furniture from family attics for our first apartment. You braided rugs: big ones, and bought antique dishes and figurines when you went on your weekly antiquing trips.

Dad, we shared music when I became a teen-ager. When I was beginning lessons, I remember hearing you call from upstairs where you were dressing to go out, "That's an E flat," or another time, "C sharp." Thank you for the hours we spent side-by-side on the piano bench playing duets. With your ability and my enthusiasm, we made beautiful music and had a lot of fun and laughs. Oh, yes, and when I'm driving, I often think of the advice you gave when you taught me how to drive, in spite of your occasional shouts to "Watch it—watch it!"

Mom and Dad, I realize today just how lucky I was to be your daughter. You had a tough time during the Depression, but you managed to provide us healthy meals and clothe us decently. I always had a new dress and new shoes at the start of each school year, and a new Easter outfit: coat, shoes and Easter bonnet. Mom, you made some of my clothes, bought some and managed to save enough from Dad's depression salary to keep us and the house looking up to date.

So thank you, Mom and Dad, for making my childhood and teen years so pleasant and for giving me the love and confidence to live a happy, fulfilled life. We never said, "I love you," but there was no need; love was always there.

Your only daughter,

Janie

December 2013

######

SEVENTEEN

By Jane Maxson

In January 1944, I celebrated my seventeenth birthday. I was a senior in high school. My life was that of a typical teen-age girl during the war years. There were basketball games, dances in the school gym and sneaking cigarettes with my friends on the north side of the building.

It was wartime and some of our older classmates had already enlisted, while the younger boys had to sign up for the draft. Ration cards limited the amount of sugar, butter and meat we could buy. Gas was rationed and cars wore A or B stickers to indicate how much gas the driver was entitled to. We even needed coupons for shoes. We walked most places or took the bus that ran between Westerly and New London.

Men in uniform were plentiful on the streets of Westerly. Soldiers stationed at Burlingame, Coast Guardsmen from the stations along the coast, and Sailors were everywhere. Our school on the hill faced the Pawcatuck River Valley and the Navy planes practicing takeoffs from the Westerly Airport came flying toward us, veering away when they seemed frighteningly close.

By June, there were only eighty-eight class members left to graduate, because so many of the boys had enlisted as soon as they were old enough. We had the traditional Flunk Day at Misquamicut where we sat on the beach or roller-skated in the casino, never realizing it was D-Day and our troops were landing in Normandy.

January, 2014

######

NEXT-DOOR NEIGHBORS
By Jane Maxson

We had lived in our house on the circle at the end of the road for two years. There were only two other houses on the street when a fourth house was built next to us on the circle We looked forward to meeting our new neighbors who introduced themselves as Gerda and Frank. They had met when Frank, actually Francisco Daniello, was in the Army in Germany. Gerda was a German war bride whose pride in her native country was frequently evident, especially when she quoted her brother who had been in the German Navy. We politely listened to Gerda's propaganda, but the war was over and we were the winners, so we let her spout.

Our first discovery that our neighbors didn't know how to get along was when Frank had someone move his driveway. The builder had curved it and Frank wanted it straight. That was OK, but when the new drive was finished, we found that it cut into a corner of our property—not much, only a few feet, but the pipe marking the property line just happened to be in the middle of the approach. We'd have agreed to it if they had asked, but there was no such request and the marker was soon covered with blacktop. I mentioned it to Frank, indicating that it might have consequences when one of the houses was sold. My first mistake.

Frank built a fence using trunks from the cedar trees that were cut when the lot was cleared. It was on his property, but the eyesore was parallel to and only feet from our driveway. When told her that rustic fences don't look right painted white. Another mistake. It wasn't painted, but the atmosphere began to chill.

I had begun substitute teaching in the local schools and one day I arrived home to find a telephone pole in the corner of my yard next to the driveway and our property line. Gerda's reply to my upset questions was that it had interfered with their driveway! I was furious but, in the interest of harmony, said little.

The Daniellos apparently thought that living in the country meant they should own a dog, so Frank and Gerda bought a pedigreed German Shepherd. The family apparently didn't really like dogs because Frank built a nice doghouse—under our bedroom window where Arco lived and barked day and night for years. I don't think the poor dog ever saw the inside of the house. Once in a while

Frank or Gerda would let Arco off his chain and he would roam up and down the road. He was a territorial dog and anyone walking on his road was in danger of being bitten. A visiting playmate of Dana's was bitten in the ankle and a boy visiting my son was nipped. I complained to Gerda. Another black mark in my book. To add to the indignity, the Daniellos bought a miniature poodle for their daughter, Debby. Heidi was housed in a doghouse next to Arco, but at least she didn't bark as much as he did.

The Daniello children were growing up and Dana, two years younger than my son, Dave, began to play with him. Gerda decided that my son was a threat to her precious Dana and no longer allowed them to play together. It was fine with me because Dana was a mean kid. His teachers told me he slyly hurt other pupils in his class.

A family with two sons around David's age moved into the last new house on the street and Dana invited them to swim in his pool. Give those boys credit; they wouldn't go unless their new friend David could go, too. Nobody went swimming that day, unless Dana swam alone.

We had a cat named Smudge, an indoor-outdoor pet. One day she disappeared. We were afraid she had been killed by a wild animal until I found her in the yard, about a week later, wet and bedraggled, with a plastic rope tied around her neck. Apparently Dana had kept Smudge tied up in his tree house. She lived for another year, then disappeared again. This time I found her in distress meowing pitifully. She was in such pain that even the trip to the vet made her cry. The vet wasn't sure what was wrong when I left her there, but I think I know. Dana had taken her again and this time really hurt her. She died that night at the vet's.

There are more stories about our neighbors like the party they invited all the neighbors to except us, their next-door neighbors. And then there's the question: did Frank have a Mafia connection? A few times men, supposedly insurance agents, came to our door asking odd questions about the Daniellos. We'll never know. He died last year in South Carolina.

October 2013

######

AN ACT OF KINDNESS
By Myrina Cardellla-Marenghi

Uncle Louis had always been kind to me, and after my father's death, he became even more so. A distant European cousin of my grandmother's, Louis, an attorney in Vienna, arrived in New York about 1920. Ostensibly, he came to research the possibility of studying in America. If he was accepted at a law school here, his wife and two young daughters would join him.

My mother's older sister Bella, married well at seventeen and shortly became pregnant. Late in the pregnancy, her husband's appendix burst during surgery, leaving her a young, beautiful, and well-off widow.

Lo and behold, a shiva visit changed Louis' life. He was hit by a thunderbolt and announced to my grandparents that, after a decent interval, he intended to marry the very pregnant Bella. They dismissed him as crazy, certain nothing more would develop. Nevertheless, Louis sailed to Europe, obtained a divorce, and true to his word, returned to New York. After the *decent interval,* he proposed to Bella. She accepted. Married, they set off on an elegant railroad journey to the west coast. After several months, they motored home across the country in a glamorous new Chrysler convertible they had purchased in California. In all, their glorious honeymoon lasted a year.

Events had moved forward so quickly, Louis had not had time to study for the bar; so he abandoned plans to attend law school. His wife's inheritance had dwindled and he had one family to support in America and another in Austria. He borrowed Bella's last few dollars to open a bedding store in America. This had been his father's trade in Europe.

Everyone in our family said Louis had hands of gold. As a hobbyist he was a gifted carpenter, he even built the elaborate miniature wooden beds on which to display lavish bedding samples in his store windows. These beds were large enough to hold dolls about two feet tall.

My mother had two sons three years apart. Then, seven years later, I was born. The January I was nine, my father died. Five months later, my oldest brother and his childhood sweetheart went ahead with their planned June wedding. Without music it was a somber affair. In September, my other brother left home to attend university upstate.

My widowed grandmother lived across the street. However, she visited us all day. One day Uncle Louis arrived with several dolls, their little carved wooden beds, and the satin quilts and canopies no longer fresh enough for his windows. Louis set up a playroom for me in my brothers' unused room. At that time, Shirley Temple was a child star and the dolls he brought were her miniature likeness.

My grandparents had considered Louis their daughter's savior when he and Bella married, conveniently overlooking the somewhat scandalous circumstances of their courtship. Now my grandmother viewed Louis as Hitler's second-in-command. All her family in Austria had perished, as had Louis' ex-wife and children. Sorrow was paralyzing, but hatred energized my grandmother. Somehow, she discovered that Louis had commandeered the entire holocaust to avoid paying child-support for his European daughters. Behind his back, she referred to him as "that heartless murderer." She never confronted Louis directly with her knowledge of his complicity, but her contemptuous attitude caused a rift between her and her daughter Bella. My mother, already overwhelmed by grief and emptiness, found herself in the midst of this new animosity. Now, in addition to her other losses, she missed the lifelong closeness she and her oldest sister had shared. I, too, sorely missed my beautiful Aunt Bella.

But my wonderful playroom enabled me to block out much of this sadness. I spent untold hours in that room, not so much playing with the dolls as retreating into a world that Louis had created for me. There, it was permissible to feel pleasure, even if only from the look and feel of the luxurious miniature satin quilts, pillows and bedspreads. Often, I just read there. Most school day afternoons I sprawled on the floor of the dolls' room to do my homework. Occasionally, I invited friends to share this oasis of glamorous ostentation in our working class Brooklyn neighborhood.

Among my contemporaries, I was notable in three respects: In a culture where everyone had two parents, I had one; I had a mother who spoke with a lovely English accent, not a strange European one, and I had this magnificent playroom.

One day, I arrived home from school to find the dolls' room empty. I assumed my mother had moved everything to wash the linoleum floor and allow it to dry. When I asked where she was keeping the dolls and their beds, my grandmother answered for her, "You're too old to still be playing with dolls. We gave them to Surala."

Surala was eight years old and had recently arrived from Europe with her parents. Her father was my grandmother's nephew and her only relative to survive the war. With Louis footing the bill—heartless, money-grubbing murderer that he was—it took years after the war ended to bring them to this country. Surala did not speak English. Truth be told, she did not speak at all. She just clung to her parents, her face usually hidden in the folds of her mother's dress. This was okay with me. Fruitlessly, my mother and grandmother attempted to explain all of Surala's past travails in Austria.

I didn't buy it. The father I adored, and who adored me, had died. My indulgent older brothers were seldom present to spoil me and make me laugh at their jokes. My mother, a cheerful woman, who often used to perform her household chores as we sang along to the kitchen radio, was now this wraith, a sad ghost of herself.

The frequent gatherings in Bella and Louis' backyard, when my handsome uncle, in his dapper Tyrolean hat, played the mandolin with his golden hands, while our entire happy family—aunts, uncles, countless cousins—sang along, had grown fewer and more far between.

I was ten years old, coping with death, loss, my grandmother's crazed sorrow, as I witnessed helplessly my beloved aunt and uncle's grief and guilt over the murders of Louis' ex-wife and daughters. My plate was full. There just was no space left for Surala, her parents, their three sets of huge, dark, haunted eyes and the stark blue numbers tattooed on the pale skin of their left arms.

One day when they visited us, Surala's father got down on his knees before me and declared, "You're such a kind little girl. You don't even know what a wonderful thing you've done by giving my Surala your dolls. You've given her back a life!"

"I don't care about Surala's life," I nearly yelled at him in front of the entire family, "I *want* my dolls back!" But of course, such as she was, this disrespectful behavior would just about have done in my grandmother, so I kept my mouth shut.

About thirty years later, my mother asked me to drive her and Bella to the unveiling of Surala's father's tombstone. After the ceremony, an old woman came over and embraced me.

Tearfully, she said, "I want you to know my husband never forgot your kindness when we came to America. He spoke about you for the rest of his life. Not many little girls would have given away such beautiful dolls to our Surala."

Can you believe, after all this time I almost screamed at this poor woman, "*I* didn't *give f**@@ **g* Surala my dolls!"

But there was my mother standing next to us, awash in the rosy memory of what a sweet child I had been. So instead, I answered her nephew's wife, "Thank you. We were honored to be able to comfort your family in some small way during that terrible time."

Now, my mother absolutely glowed like a plum because that generous child she remembered, had grown up to become such a gracious woman.

######

A Moment in Time

By Jack Barry

On a slow November day, last milking done, a handful of locals gather in Donal Kane's pub to knock back a pint or two and do what Irish do best. Talk. Too many full pints of Guinness lined up in front of me, bought by men who still remember my mother fifty years back. I'm trying to figure out how to deal with these tributes when I hear a keening. The flat nasal cry turns to melody as the hum of soft Kerry accents stops, giving the room to the music. The music is coming from a young man who looks to be in his twenties. You can see by his ruddy face and strong hands he spends most of his time out in the West Ireland winter wind. His voice is as clear and sweet as the old Gaelic lament he sings will allow. When the last note is sung the room stays silent a moment. Finally an old timer turns to the young man "Stout lad!" Others nod. Then, along with the young man, they return to their talk. The silence, that lasts but for a moment, is with me forever.

######

OK City
By Jack Barry

So here I am after half a day of hitchhiking, sitting on a bench in a little park in downtown Oklahoma City under the blank-eyed gaze of Wiley Post. Wiley was a famous 1930s barnstorming pilot who, as the plaque says, flew into eternity (really a lagoon in Alaska) with his good friend, humorist, Will Rogers.

I'm here because, after months of standard Army delay, I finally got a weekend pass and a chance to get off post. It's Saturday and it takes a while to hitch my first ride.

"Where ya' headed?"

"Oklahoma City."

"I can only take ya' to the next wah."

"What the hell is a wah? Damn! This is gonna' take me all weekend." As it turns out a Y is where a road splits and the next one is forty miles away. There's a half-pint bottle of Wild turkey on the passenger seat. The driver takes the bottle and, one handed, deftly half fills a Dixie cup propped between his legs and offers me a drink. It's still morning and besides I don't see another cup handy so, "No thanks." I do believe I'm going to like Oklahoma after all.

A few benches away a guy is killing a bottle in a paper bag. Welcome to the Bible belt. I casually pat my pockets—big bills in the right; singles in the left. I figure sooner or later he's going to hit me up for some money. Sure enough! He takes a deep breath sort of storing up the hot air that's coming and shuffles over. "Excuse me sir..."

Sir? I'm a skinny twenty-year-old kid with a bad GI haircut. Who does he think he's fooling?

"Excuse me sir. My name is Max Biermann. I'm trying to get back home to Ponca City. I got a job waiting. Could you please help me out?"

"No, but tell you what. I'll go a couple of bucks and we share the next bottle. Ok?"

While we're knocking off the bottle of cheap wine I learn that Max just got out of the city jail that morning. In OK City back then, Public Vagrancy gets you five days or five dollars. In 1972 the Supreme Court found such laws to be too vague but that was too late to help Max. Max got out after four days because a cellmate named Smiley passed the hat and got the dollar Max needed to get released early. There are no Sunday releases so Max would not have gotten out until Monday. Max learns that I'm on a weekend pass from Fort Sill, don't much like the Army, haven't got a room for the night yet, and my father is a drunk.

We make a plan. Max will wire his boss for twenty-five bucks on the promise he'll show up for work Monday morning. When the money comes, Max will use three dollars to bail Smiley out of the can and the three of us will rent a room, knock back a few and have a good old time. So down to the Western Union office to send the telegram off to Ponca City. That done, we buy another bottle to shorten the wait. The wine is beginning to take its toll. But, we stick to the plan, and after a blurry couple of hours, we head back to the Western Union office.

"Howdy Little Lady!"

The girl behind the Western Union counter reminds me of that American Gothic picture only younger and without the pitchfork; but every bit as severe, right down to the painful looking part in the middle of her head. Her nose keeps twitching. I think she's afraid she might get drunk on our fumes.

"I mean morning Ma'am." (It's late afternoon.)

"You got some money for Max Bierman?"

She slowly opens a drawer on the other side of the counter like she's expecting snakes to leap out and slither up her pale arms. She takes her time studying the one piece of paper in the drawer. Without answering Max's question she keeps her eyes on the piece of paper and asks. "Do you have any identification, sir?"

Max looks slack mouthed confused. She smiles a bland little victory smile. Then Max smiles—real wide—and leans on the counter. She takes a half step back. Max leans closer. She takes a full step to the left. It's like some kind of dance. Max throws his head back, thrusts his arm in the air flamenco style, pulls a full upper plate out of his mouth, leans further over the counter, and palm up, offers his teeth to the young girl.

"Ya' see these teeth Ma'am? Got them in the US Navy. See! That's my USN and there's my name M. Biermann. These teeth won't fit anyone else's mouth but mine—unless you want to give it a try honey."

A quick step backward. Her eyes wide. Her part even seems wider now. Twenty-five bucks are thrown on the counter. I can see Max is beginning to enjoy this little encounter. With a flourish, he signs off for the money. I scoop it up and steer him out the door.

Given our condition when we go to spring Smiley, we're lucky we don't get arrested at the jail. I have all I can do to keep Max's teeth in his goddamn mouth. It's like he discovered a key to the city or something. The cop on the desk is laid back and bored, but even his nose twitches a bit. Looks like he could use a drink. Smiley is a grizzled old cowboy with a chew stained beard. I like him.

We head for the flophouse. Jennette, the woman behind the desk has a smokers face and a road map of varicose veins exposed below a shapeless housedress. You get the feeling she hasn't smiled in a long time. She leads us up three flights and throws back a curtain that serves as a door. There is one bed with a thin suspicious looking mattress, a couple of wooden chairs, and a dirty sink with a missing hot water tap. The hopper and shower are down the hall. Jennette comes back with a few scrawny blankets and throws them on the bed.

"Alright boys! No fights. No fires. No screwing around. Understand?"

When she leaves Max walks over to the sink and pisses in it. I'm not sure if he really has to relieve himself or whether he's just marking territory. Smiley wants to get down to business and volunteers to go get the hooch. He returns in a short time with a gallon jug of Wild Irish Rose.

"Stronger than Thunderbird and all that other crap." he says. With him are two guys he met in jail earlier in the week. Smiley opens the bottle with a flourish and with a big smile introduces Thomas and William. They throw a little money onto the bed. I don't know it yet but this will be the high point of the evening; anticipating a night with an unlimited supply of booze.

After the bottle is passed around a few times a skinny, no ass, big belt buckle dude stumbles in. "Howdy folks! I'm Jim from across the hall. Looks like y'all got a nice little party goin'. Mind if I join?"

No one says yeah but no one says no. Jim throws a few coins on the bed, takes a couple of long swigs out of the bottle, belches as if that's part of the drinking deal and passes it to me. I am well past needing another swig and wave him off

"No thanks."

Jim gives me a look. "Who's the kid?"

Max takes the bottle. "This is Jack. He's ok. His daddy's a man of the road too."

I didn't know I had a pedigree. Maybe everyone has one, one way or another. Max starts to pass the bottle on to Thomas.

Jim now gives Thomas a look. "You an Indian?"

"Yeah?"

"I knew it. A Cherokee. Am I right?

"What's it to you little man?"

"I don't drink with Cherokees especially when they're drunk!"

Thomas slowly gets to his feet, William right behind him. Jim stumbles back and pulls a puny little jackknife, waving it back and forth. "Call off your dogs!"

Max grabs the jug by the neck and steps between the men and hisses, "Get the hell out!"

Jim backs toward the door still waving the knife. "Screw you guys! I have a bottle of real whiskey, not the shit you and Tonto there been drinking."

With that he shuffles out.

Smiley turns to Thomas and William. "That's one troubled hombre. Have another drink amigo."

I think at that moment Smiley wishes he could speak Cherokee.

What stuck in my mind was how fast all these guys got drunk, how fast and ugly they crashed and how much schoolyard shit went on. I started to see my father in a different light.

The next morning, head banging and stomach churning, I ease past the snoring bodies and head for Fort Sill. Walking toward the highway with my thumb out, a hot red sports car zips by and screeches to a stop a ways up the road. Sometimes when this happens you run up the road so your ride doesn't have to wait, only to have the asshole peel out when you're almost to the car. So I'm grateful the stop was real.

"Hey man, thanks for stopping.

The driver, Hal, shakes my hand "Where you headed?"

"Lawton."

"You're in luck. I'm headed to Anadarko"

I am in luck. I always try to make conversation figuring whoever picks me up is bored and could use some company. Hal is an ABD (all but dissertation) epidemiologist studying venereal disease among Native American males. He is amazed that I'm familiar with Hans Zinsser's book "Rats Lice and History." (I don't tell him I only bought it because of the title.) The main point of the book is we're creating super germs that survive 1000 degree steam in hospital laundries, flies that get fat on DDT, virus permutations from China for which there is no vaccine. Meanwhile. Public health programs keep people in the gene pool who would have died young in a more Darwinian environment. The conclusion? A pandemic is just a matter of time.

He absolutely cackles when I tell him about my "Cracked Plate Theory," which states that according to many old wives, cracks in plates harbor deadly germs. Therefore, in order to keep our gene pool filled with folks blessed with tough no nonsense white blood cell warriors we should all eat off cracked plates and let Darwin have his way. I was hoping this conversation might get me all the way to Fort Sill but it was not to be.

When we get to Chickasha, I realize hitchhiking would be better from Chickasha than from Anadarko and you can only talk about rats, lice, and even history for so long.

As we pull up to the one traffic light in town, I grab my duffle bag, start to thank Hal and open the car door. He looks surprised and reaches across the seat. I reach out to shake his hand but he grabs for my crotch. I jump out of the car.

Everything happened so fast. But standing by the road waiting for the next ride, I think about how naïve I am. I mean the guy had a polished wood penis on his stick shift. Am I dumb or what? On the way back to post, I'm thinking about my father and what I learned this weekend about his life or lack of it. I know he's smarter than those guys in OK City but I'm thinking in a lot of ways I'm older than he is or more like he's younger than I am.

######

Odyssey

By Jack Barry

Jane tapped a cigarette from the pack and felt for her lighter. *I'll give her this last smoke then I'm out of here.*

A white Honda Odyssey pulled into the parking lot. Jane quickly stuffed the unlit cigarette into her coat pocket and smiled. *Jesus! Afraid of getting caught smoking in a church parking lot. I must really be going off the deep end!*

The car pulled up alongside Jane. The driver was a plump, fortyish woman with perfect hair, botoxed face and white Burberry coat. When she rolled down her window, Jane became aware of the Dolce & Gabbana fragrance, Light Blue.

"You must be Jane."

Jane didn't know the perfume but knew money when she smelled it. "Yeah, I'm Jane. I hope you're Gladys".

A nervous little chuckle then a loud "Lord Jane! I hope I am too."

Jane thought, *I don't know anything about cars but I do know this lady has been well taken care of and the car is about as spotless as her coat.* Jane already knew she was going to buy the car, but figured it would be best to go through the negotiating routine. At $8,500 it was a steal.

"So Gladys, why are you selling the car?"

"Well, my husband George has been transferred overseas. Paris no less."

"Wow! You must be so excited!"

"You know Jane, I'm not so sure."

"Not so sure?"

"Oh, I know they have good food and nice art over there but I've been told that men relieve themselves in broad daylight and beggars actually touch you and then there's the funny language-like they all have sinus infections. I'm just not so sure."

"Any problems with the car that you know of Gladys?"

"We always brought the car in promptly for all its inspections and so forth. Brand new tires too. All the receipts are in the glove compartment. I numbered each one by date. Would you like to see them?"

"No Gladys, I believe you."

"Oh wait! There was one thing. They somehow couldn't find a way to fix no matter how many times I told them. I do want to make sure I've been totally honest with you"

"What was that Gladys?"

"Well the driver's seat belt occasionally gets in the way when you try to close the door. What a racket! I'm afraid something's going to break. I brought it to three different dealers but they all said it's just the way it was designed and there wasn't anything they could do. Just make sure it's inside the car when you close the door they said. I actually thought of writing to Mr. Honda or whoever"

"Jesus!" Jane thought, "let's get on with this. Well, Gladys, I like your car and I'm prepared to offer you $6,500 cash."

Gladys said a weak but quick OK and looked relieved. 'You know, Jane, this is the first time I did anything like this. I was so nervous—Craigslist and all that. George made me do it. Said negotiating would be good training for France. I don't know. You never know whom you're going to be dealing with. Is there a Craigslist in France? I'm glad it was you. You really seem to know what you're doing."

"I like you too, Gladys. Oh—one more thing before we take care of business." Jane took a tape measure and measured the distance from behind the driver's seat to the rear hatch. She thought, *it's a bit short but I can always put his body in on a diagonal, or maybe saw his legs if needed.* "OK Gladys let's get this show on the road."

As soon as Jane got back to her apartment she called Danny. "Hey Danny. I got us a car for the job."

"Jane, what did I tell ya'? What did I godamn tell ya'—huh!"

"Not to use the phone. Sorry, Dan, I forgot."

"See you in half an hour at the office, Jane."

The office was a bar called Panacea where you could spend a lot of time just reading tattoos. Danny liked this intrigue stuff. Liked it almost as much as he liked killing people. Jane knew she could never kill anyone but was surprised at how the game excited her. And, the pay wasn't bad. Wasn't bad at all. And this one will be the biggest payday yet. Danny was in touch with the client, a lady with deep pockets—very deep pockets. She wanted her husband out of the way in the worst way and was clearly willing to pay. She knew her husband trolled certain Internet sites. She knew what he liked.

Jane is the bait; complete with outrageous red stiletto heels and a demure Sunday hat. A call girl with a wide range of desires, imagination, and technique who will put this John in heaven. The plan is to get the John tied up in a bit of bondage foreplay. Danny shows up as the irate husband; shoots the John; plants some meth; loads the body in the Odyssey, meets the client at the river to inspect the job and pay for services rendered. Then we dump the body. Simple!

Well not exactly! Everything's going smoothly. Jane enjoys a second glass of wine. Danny bursts into the room before anyone's tied up. He raises the gun to shoot the John. The long silencer on the barrel hits the nightstand. The bullet goes through the fleshy part of the John's thigh. For a pudgy little guy he's quick and strong. He grabs the pistol by the long silencer and slowly turns it on Danny. Danny starts to whimper. Jane thinks she sees the John smile. Another shot. Danny teeters, looking surprised that he has a hole in his forehead, then falls across the John knocking him to the floor. Jane understands she's in a world of hurt. Without thinking she grabs her red shoe and swings with all her might. Slowly sinking to the carpet the John looks almost as surprised as Danny, blood gushing from behind his ear.

Jane doesn't know how she ever got those bodies in the Odyssey. Must be adrenaline. By the time she gets to the river she's shaking—exhausted. She pulls up next to a large Mercedes. The window rolls down. Jane catches a familiar scent of expensive perfume. The client leans out the window.

"Gladys! What are you doing here?"

"Lordy, Jane I was about to ask you the same thing."

"Gladys, I need your help."

"Well Jane, let's get this show on the road"

######

Stirring

By Ann Kelsey Thacher

She stands by the stove silently
stirring
the oatmeal for the kids who fill her day.

Her feet and body don't yet ache, yet.
Later,
her whole self will complain of the chores.

Her mind is set free to roam by repetitive
stirring.
It releases her thoughts, and they soar.

The early time quiet prompts her to feel herself.
Alone
is a balm for her neglected intellect.

She hears whimpers and she knows the baby's
stirring
Baby trumps oatmeal. So she goes.

Later in the day, she has another
moment,
older children in school, baby sleeping.

She puts on music from now distant youth. It's
stirring.
Another time for thoughts to seize her.

Poetry, she finds, is written in her head.
recording
it is what there is no time for.

She looks at her watch; it's time for children to be
stirring
the silence , streaming in the door with tales of school.

The house feels warmer, fuller now,
expanding
with the joy of small ones back from the world.

It's difficult for her to accept that the
stirring
of her young children is all she needs now.

######

Do You Remember Seventeen?

By Dorothy Devine

In 1964 I was a junior at New Trier High School on Chicago's North Shore. I won a spot in a program called the Summer Seminar in Community Affairs, which was organized by two social studies teachers. This was an experience in integration, as the only non-whites at our high school were a foreign student from Ethiopia and several children of live-in servants from the Woodley Road neighborhood of millionaires like the Wrigleys (of chewing gum and Wrigley Field).

In my application essay I wrote of the opportunities to improve human relations, become a better writer, broaden my experience, and participate in social action. I expressed excitement at the idea that Chicago problems could be solved by looking at the entire urban area and things like housing discrimination, bank red-lining, and white flight as part of the problem. I quoted TO KILL A MOCKINGBIRD's author Harper Lee saying you couldn't understand another person until "you climb into his skin and walk around in it."

For six weeks, our group of teenagers from the comfortable suburbs and the prize-winning high school with its Olympic-sized swimming pool and the professional stage (which had launched Rock Hudson, Charlton Heston, and Ann-Margaret), was paired with an equal number of "Negro" students from city high schools, who had been chosen by their school principals.

We toured suburban villages and the inner city on a bus, then on foot, visited white, black, middle class, working class and poor neighborhoods. We met with town managers and social workers, realtors, the famous Jackie Robinson, urban community organizers, and academics. We studied the Constitution, articles on white flight and housing discrimination, and works on the causes of poverty.

Most afternoons we worked together on service projects: painting walls in a settlement house, conducting a city housing-use survey, cleaning broken glass from a playground, planting flowers around a community clinic.

The city students were invited to a pool party at one of our residences, and I and several other white girls went to a sleepover at the home of a black girl whose father was a Chicago police detective. There was a girl who lived in a South Side housing project and I remember how frightened our teacher was walking into the project to escort her back to her door after dark.

I was paired with Willy, a tall gentle fatherless boy from another housing project, to go door to door in Elmhurst to do a housing survey. As we walked through the hot July neighborhoods, we held hands. We never hugged or kissed, but he did come home for dinner.

Were any of our lives changed? The tall young man attended Oberlin College and eventually, briefly, was married to a white woman. My father, a Navy reservist, helped the detective's son apply to the Navy. I became painfully aware that my relative ease and huge amount of opportunity was part of the problem. The other progressive white students took me along to my first Pete Seeger concert and we sang freedom songs all the way home on the train. My best girlfriend traveled to register voters in Mississippi at the end of the summer and saw a black teen in her team shot dead as he walked across a gas station parking lot.

My strongest impressions are of a street fair where we had a table about our project when some black kids pulled one of the white boys from our group and beat him to the ground. I fled to a nearby church bathroom and wept inconsolably for a very long time. Only years later did my mother tell me that both the black police detective and my father worked the fair that day, both packing guns, hoping to keep everyone safe.

By the following spring, filled with fear for his only daughter, my dad began calling my friends "riffraff," my ideals "ridiculous." We struggled so long and loudly that, still unkissed, I moved out right after high school graduation and never lived home or in the Chicago area again.

6 February 2014

######

EXPERIMENT WITH PARENTHESES

By Dorothy Devine

My mother (first love in every culture) died nine years
ago today
I plan a liquid fast (for mental clarity and cleansing)
Death is underlined by a wren trapped by my "squirrel-
    proof" feeder (squirrels know if they jump atop, the
    seeds will fall to the ground)
Maybe it was the high wind (I'm not sure why); the
    feeder closed and the wren's neck was broken
    (instantly I hope)
I see she has a tiny millet seed in her beak when I place
    her gently in the woods (I am planning millet in my
    morning meal tomorrow when I break this fast).

I walk my terrier our usual three miles (up the street,
    behind the school, on the bike path, through the
    woods)
She finds another bird in the leaves (this time a robin)
    and death again is underlined
I send a blessing skyward for both birds' spirits (the
    spring sky is an astonishing blue)
I think of Mom again (at 89, death for her was
    liberation)
Does she watch her children, or is she glad to be free of
    us (especially when we hurt and anger one another)?

I teach an elders' class where I lead safe exercises
    (encouraging "2P"s today: Pep and Posture)
My reward: Qi Gong class (led by Tony, I can be a
    student)
Breathing deeply, sending healing inward, filling myself
    with calm (need to work on my balance)
Eager to get outside in the beautiful day with my terrier
    (this time for a shorter walk, no death discovered)
My real plan for today is the garden (compost for the

hosta, more cleanup of the brush-filled borders).
Nine years ago my brother Phil and I buried Mom's
ashes in the back yard near the pond (I add compost to
the sweet woodruff planted at the spot.)

I also sit on the cedar bench, resting and talking to her
    (should she choose to hear me)
I tell her I am slimmer and healthier than I have ever
    been (the cancer has stayed away)
I am going to the same writers' group she once
    attended (although the group leader has changed)
In two days, I am reading one of my written pieces
    publicly (for the very first time) at a local library.

I've already talked about retiring and getting married
    (if she listened)
I tell her I am happy and at peace (comfortable, safe,
    untroubled)
I'll talk to her again on her birthday (less than a month
    away)
She knew I saw her in myself all the time (the
    thoughtful and helpful parts of me)
She was a late blooming author (now, perhaps I'll be
    one, too).

My mother (first love in every culture) died nine years
    ago today.
I filter my water (with a blender I can drink four fruits,
    four vegetables, two kinds of nuts)
I fill my lungs with fresh air (think of life and death)
Surround myself with what makes me grateful (home,
    sweet love, loyal friends, little dogs)
My mother (first love in every culture) died nine years
    ago today.

25 April 2014

######

— 43 —

May You Live In Interesting Times

By Dorothy Devine

Asked why I write, I have to reply that I write to see if I have learned anything. With a life over the last fifty years very different from the one my grandparents, parents and brothers, and especially my mother expected me to have, what were the good lessons? What are still questions? Do I understand more or less of the world? I write to improve and explore my self-awareness.

My genre of choice for these explorations is descriptive non-fiction. I strive to tell the truth as I understood it: about myself, what I did, where I went, what I saw, how I survived. My interesting times began in the sixties, spanned the seventies and eighties, and continued into the new millennium. While each in our Thursday morning group had her or his own curse or opportunity of interesting times -- London during the blitz, war-time Germany, and others -- my particular journey is that of a twentieth-century American woman with many choices. I fell from privilege to modest means, from idealism to fecklessness, from a sheltered world to what many may consider losing my way. I moved 33 times between the ages of 17 and 33, and my first home of my own was a teepee I sewed from about $200 worth of sailcloth. A very late-bloomer, I finally learned how to survive, to simplify, to help myself, and to recognize beauty and courage all around me.

I want to write about a journey from teenage civil rights advocate to college anti-war activist to guest worker in Fidel Castro's Cuba. The journey took me from college professor's runaway wife to troubled wanderer with a hippie name and no sustaining work. I want to write about the families I forged with others equally rejecting of (or rejected by) their birth families, the promises we made and broke, the bottoms we hit, and the dangers we survived (and in some cases did not survive). I want to be honest about some things that may be uncomfortable or remind others of fears they had for their own children during similar times.

Looking for some who attempted similar projects, I found Tom Hayden, a founder of Students for a Democratic Society, wrote a memoir of these times called REUNION. Peter Coyote, an actor who was in the San Francisco Mime Troupe, wrote one called SLEEPING WHERE WE FALL. My world was certainly a mix of the two they describe. But these are men, and men in those times had very different lives, as throughout history, than did women.

What I hope to gather from the Thursday morning group is enough suspension of judgment to allow for criticism of the language and the level of clarity. Is what I am saying understandable? Do I move beyond self-absorption to learning? Do I capture the spirit of the times I describe or am I still too much of an outsider? Do I need to self-censor to be more accessible?

######

19 February 2014

THEN AND NOW

By Dorothy Devine

THEN:

In the reception hall, the student agency servers exclaimed, "All the Students for a Democratic Society are here!" remembering the recent building takeovers and angry Cambridge police. The bride's brother and the groom discussed Marxism. The bride's mother could not hear what anyone said because her daughter kept turning up the music, resetting it to the Rolling Stones singing, "Let's drink to the hard working people; Let's think of the lowly of birth. Let's drink to the two thousand million; Let's think of the humble of birth. Spare a thought for the rag-taggy people; Let's drink to the salt of the earth..."

The mother-of-the-bride wondered why it all felt so wrong. They had hoped for peace, too, until her husband enlisted after Pearl Harbor. He had cut off financial support to their daughter, which meant she juggled work in an insurance agency with her last two years of college. Her daughter's "A" average made her hope she was OK. Why did body language telegraph anger? Why did the groom's parents seem so embarrassed? Was her daughter pregnant? Or was she just too busy keeping the young man's bed warm and his apartment clean to know what she wanted to do with her life besides hating war and poverty? Didn't we all hate war and poverty?

None of either set of parents' friends or relatives attended. The student-agency photographer took grainy black and white pictures, many out of focus. The bride changed into another mini-dress, and as she climbed into the car borrowed for her honeymoon on the Cape, the headache she had all day intensified and she wondered why she was actually married to someone who, three years after meeting him, already bored her.

NOW:

The two women had known one another for 33 years and lived together for 31. The five-and nine-year-olds the younger woman had when they met towered over them both, an amazing 39 and 42 years old. Because laws had changed, they could legally marry in their state and better protect one another as they aged, and especially if one survived the other. The older bride had trouble locating her 1972 divorce decree from BC—before computers—and the ceremony was delayed.

They had felt married since the mid-1980s, but now no parents survived to attend. A small group of long-time friends decorated their home with garlands and white flowers, carried in food and drink, witnessed, officiated, and celebrated with them the success of their long relationship, rather than a new beginning. Tears were nonetheless shed as the reverend recounted the challenges they had faced: at times troubled sons, cancer treatment a few short years apart, and continuous care-giving for limited or aging and dying relatives. Triumphs celebrated were education, careers, gardens, vacations in the West, community, and creativity in the form of music, stained glass, and writing.

The younger bride picked up one of the many guitars crowding the room and sang her vows. The older bride's vows were spoken haltingly, with many pauses for deep breaths. She mentioned her gratitude at never once being bored.

######

Wish Dreams

By Reinhard Fröhlich

The assignment was: "You begin to notice that whatever you write seems to come true."

If I know that if whatever I write becomes true, I doubt you would like to read what I would write down. I would write about my wildest dreams. It would be awesome, morally destructive, insulting and simply impossible. Particularly one member, Monica, would be furious throwing whatever she has nearby at me. It would be the end of my stint at the Neighborhood Guild Writer's Group. I may even have to appear in court. No, no, I better abandon this project.

Instead let me tell you about a life-long dream that seems to become true very soon. I remember the first book I read, a beautiful book. I must have been seven years old. It was about a small house nicely located in a dense wood. The railway line went by and the owner was the gatekeeper. He didn't have much to do, as the express train went by only twice a day, one coming and the other going to and from the big city that was far away. But it was important that the gates were down when a train came by at high speed. The description of the wood with singing birds, rabbits, foxes, and other animals made me envious—yes I would like to live in such a house in the wood. I dreamed ever since of the wood, at day and at night.

At that time I grew up in Potsdam, a beautiful town founded by Frederick the Great. Once Father took us out to Wild Park, a nearby wood, where the King went for a hunt. I loved it; will I ever live in such a wood? Then there was war, the invasion of the Russian army and flight to West Germany. There was in front of me the Teutoburger Forest, a huge wood. We lived in a farmhouse surrounded by cornfields. I spent many hours, days and weeks in the forest hiking and resting and admiring the trees. The close succession of war, Russian occupation, and the lean years were a lot for a thirteen year old to digest. Actually I didn't digest it at all, I guess. Imagine you sit in a cinema for ten hours looking at all kinds of Schwarzenegger's films. You switch off and start dozing. I needed time in the forest to calm down. It was like a meditation after which I was ready for new adventures. However, my dream of a house in the woods became stronger and stronger. Then I lived in all the big cities: Bonn, Mainz, Duesseldorf, Karlsruhe and London. Yes there were parks, but I kept dreaming of my house in the woods.

Finally in Rhode Island I am almost there. We live in the *OAKS*. The house is surrounded by trees, but we do not live in the woods yet. Here I learn what I did not read in the book, or I may have forgotten it. I have to rake leaves every fall. Once there were very few leaves when we had the gypsy moth. I love these little animals and I don't understand why most people don't like them. Oaks are quite useless trees, as their leaves are acidic and not good for the soil. Besides their blossoms are slimy, which is particularly annoying if they stick to your window.

Soon I may come to the fulfillment of my recurring dream and live in a real wood in the western part of Maine near Portland. There are no oaks and there will be very little leaf raking. If the ground is covered with pine needles you think you walk on a soft carpet. It will not be a little house like in the book. It is a large mansion with many rooms, where you can get lost. But eventually I will find my way. My son, the master of the castle, the "Burggraf", will help us to adjust. Moral of this story: keep dreaming over and over again and your dream will finally become true. Of course, the dream must be reasonable; don't dream of a Mercedes or Rolls Royce!

5 June 2014

######

THE BLIZZARD OF FRIDAY NIGHT

By Reinhard Fröhlich

In the middle of the night I open the door to listen what is going on outside. Nothing but snow and it is quiet. Then I hear a train coming by and a tree creaking. That is a twister, as I was told later. Not good and I close the door. The lights go out—no electricity—which means we also have no heat. Tonight we will still be OK. The next morning we are on another planet. Two trees came down and landed exactly between the garage, my canoe, and the barbecue grill; there was no damage. We thanked the angels who directed them so precisely; they were professionals.

I look up into a strange world of frozen trees; they are covered with snow and ice and the branches are hanging down, some half broken. A fir tree is hanging down as if it wanted to kiss the ground. They show no sign of life; they are dead. The touch of death is so beautiful. Then I look into the sky and it is not beautiful at all. Dark patches of clouds move by very fast. Some are brighter, some darker. No sun but some light comes through the brighter clouds so you can guess where the sun should be. I am mesmerized...

Yes, it was a bitter cold winter. But we had heat in Soviet Occupied Germany. We looted wood from the bombed out houses; the most yielding place was the former rowing club. We had a 'Kachelofen', a large oven with tiles that was our life support. Food was difficult to get. We were lucky to have powdered cheese. Mix it with water and you had quark, some sort of cottage cheese without the little knots. It was good, but we had it for two months, every morning and evening. On the black market, Mother had swapped her boots for this. After she received the cheese, she ran away hoping it would take some time until the Russian woman discovered the boots had a slit at one side and would probably be of no use to her. The cheese will last another month. We gnawed our teeth for the monotony but, at the same time, were thankful to get something of substance into our stomachs for one more month.

"Come in," my wife Patricia calls me, "you cannot stand there, it is cold".

Slowly I turn to her. She comes out and takes my arm.

"You are cold," she says, "quickly come". I return from my journey to the past.

"It was a cold winter," I say, "people were dying in the cold, particularly the old ones. Frau Mielke's older sister, a colleague of my Father, was found dead one morning in her bed. "

"Oh, you remember," says Patricia.

"Yes the winter of 1947 was a bad one."

"Sit down, you are all cold, I make you a whisky, a left-over from the Irish pudding," she encourages me to come back to Rhode Island.

"Yes, the winter of 1947 I will never forget."

8 February 2013

######

MY FIRST JOB IN AMERICA

By Reinhard Fröhlich

The monotony of the German civil service was a bit depressing and boring, though quite frankly my job was anything but monotonous. But the desire to explore the wide world had grabbed me like a big vise at my ankle, preventing me from making big steps in Germany. After a lengthy exchange of letters with a powerful, knowledgeable man in Missouri we obtained a visa, arrived in New York, and continued to St. Louis. Moving along in a rented car we were heading for Rolla.

"Rolla—next five exits," says a road sign.

"Must be a big place, "I said.

"Well, we just take off when we see the skyscrapers of the university," I continued.

According to the description my future boss, the Dean, gave of the university, there had to be skyscrapers, the essence of America. Well, there were none and at exit no.5 we left the highway. Somewhere on a road I asked where Rolla is. "This is it," a man said.

My wife and I looked into each other's eyes. "This is it?"

My official title was Associate Professor and Director of the Geophysical Observatory. "So where is my staff?" I asked one day.

Heads were shaking. Then I was brought to the Observatory, a seismic station recording earthquakes located in a cave in the wilderness. The station was a mess; you thought a bomb went off to destroy it. Later I learned that geophysicists of St Louis University had a big grant to establish a seismic network in the Midwest to monitor Soviet Nuclear Explosions. The Russians were suspected to set off explosions in earthquake prone areas. They sort of smuggled their nuclear blasts in-between their earthquakes. When the grant to St. Louis University had expired, the station was donated to UMR, the University of Missouri at Rolla. I gave it my best to get it back into "running mode," which included janitorial cleanup, testing, calibration, and so forth. St. Louis University was not too far for visits and advice. They were pleased to occasionally receive my records and they invited me to give a talk. Nearby is the famous/infamous New Madrid earthquake zone in the southeastern tip of Missouri. There, the most damaging earthquake in the USA in

1814 occurred. I was expected to bring in funding for the seismic station. That was almost impossible since analyzing the records was not a fundable project.

The university didn't seem to have any structure. Some of the professors had a farm that didn't quite support them, so they had to take on another job to make ends meet. Teaching geology at UMR came in handy.

I was deeply disappointed. They didn't seem to have any notion of "teamwork" and in more than one case I was warned not to talk about my ideas if so-and-so was present. They would run away with it and write a proposal. This was some zoo. It turned out that my boss, the Dean, knew little about geophysics and many thought he was a mediocre geologist. But he was a good Mormon, a bishop. One day I discovered that my budget had been severely slashed. The Mormon Dean shifted money from the Observatory to his Mormon friend, a Professor of Biology. I was furious, as I needed the money to run the observatory. Somehow the Mormons have a practical touch with money. Promote a Mormon fellow and he earns more money, so part of it ends in the coffers of their church. Some of the most ridiculous people became eventually full professor.

I needed daily six pieces of photo paper about 12 by 60 inches from Kodak. So far my records were good and often requested by the US Geological Survey if there was an earthquake or nuclear explosion they were interested in. The next year our sloshed funds allowed us to record until the end of April—then what?

I was devastated and told my assistant, also a Mormon, but one of the few good ones I came across: "Karl, there has to be a miracle! You pray to your Mormon God, I will pray to my Protestant God, who may still know me, and my wife will pray to the Catholic God, who is a powerful one; ask for a miracle regarding recording paper."

One day the people from Kodak brought the cartons of film and we showed them where to pile them up. Finally I thought we had enough and the two guys would say good-bye or let me sign a slip. They brought more and kept coming. My assistant Karl was going to alert them that they gave us too much, when I put my hand on his arm and told him that this is the miracle. The angels from Kodak did a fine job supplying us with a full year's recording paper. You may think this is funny; I don't. I believe in the power of sincere prayer.

And they never recognized any mistake or asked for more money or for a return of the excess paper. No this was a genuine miracle.

There were many bizarre incidents and eventually I was funded for two groundwater projects, one about the famous caves in the karst. They were soon published. In the end I even got a grant in conjunction with the seismic station. That was enough to establish myself in the USA. All in all, Missouri was an interesting experience but not for the long run. After four years I came to URI. Sometimes I go back in my dreams, canoeing on the Current River, visiting Mark Twain's house (or Tom Sawyer's) in Hannibal, the Missouri River, and free running land turtles.

After the marvelous performance of the angels from Kodak, I wondered why did the Good Lord send me to Missouri? Now God does not give me straight answers, he lets me find out for myself. This happened in the library of URI. Before we came to America I suffered at the time of our marriage a bad backache, caused by a slipped disk. This was related to fieldwork in the unhealthy climate of the Lower Rhine—wet and cold. For three weeks I lay flat in bed. When I eventually recovered, the doctor said he never saw somebody like me recovering so fast from my injury. But he warned me not to lift anything heavy and I may arrive home in my car to find out I cannot move. I must be carried up the stairs.

27 February 2014

######

LETTER FROM THE OTHER WOMAN

By Barbara Reynolds

Ms. Arabella Puffington   740 Park Avenue
New York, NY

Mrs. Cora Van Lent
1 Corn Cob Lane
Poughkeepsie, New York

Dear Cora,

I found your address in Ted's wallet; can you ever forgive me for taking him away from you? One month seems like an eternity when I realize how you and the children must feel.

Would it be possible for you to come to my apartment tomorrow night about 6? And please bring the children, all five of them. Perhaps Ted would have an attack of conscience when he saw their sweet faces longing for his return.

The evening that I picked Ted up at the county fair was completely out of character for me. Generally I choose my men from the corporate field and I research my options quite well. Ted never let on he was married let alone that he was a father of five. How could I know that his story of being related to an old oil family was completely fabricated? Do you think that his father's gas station in the Bronx makes him qualify as being in oil? Anyhow by the time I found out about you and his children he had moved into my Park Avenue apartment. He claimed that he didn't need a job because of the large deposits by his family into his checking account each month. I was so busy with my start up company of matching singles online that I failed to notice that he spent his entire day in the library. He claimed that he was doing research for a non-profit owned by his family. After a while I realized that I was becoming a non-profit also. Ted hated to talk about money; he said it was so crass. And finally I realized that our dear Ted hated to talk about money because he didn't have any.

Although he has adapted quite well to my fourth floor penthouse, I think he misses you and the children in your rural setting. I really want to do the right thing by you and the children.

I will alert my doorman to your arrival tomorrow night at 6pm.

Remorsefully Yours,
Arabella Puffington

######

ROSES ON RAYON

By Barbara Reynolds

Roses on rayon and eyelet with ribbons.

Cashmere and challis with sparkly sequins.

Satin and silk catching light in their folds

Shimmering velvets of ivory and gold.

When the dawn comes in with malice.

Spilling chills and grey.

I try to remember these glorious gowns.

And then I can keep all the gloom away.

######

THE DOORS OF JOY-THE DOORS OF GLOOM

By Barbara Reynolds

The White church door is open
The organ trills a hum.
I gather folds of taffeta
My journey has begun.
Beguiled by mounds of roses
And lilts of songs of grace
The white door closes soundlessly
I am inside and safe.
Today the door I open
To get inside the room
Is massive, dark and ugly
With mustiness and gloom.
The vows I made in hopeful voice
Have come to be denied.
The doors of life are pushed both ways
Some welcome and some grey.
The edicts signed, the deed is done
No turning back today.

######

KINDNESS

By David Barwise

The writer, Ella Wilcox, has expressed KINDNESS this way:

So many gods, so many creeds,
So many paths that wind and wind,
While just the art of being kind
Is all the sad world needs.

We live in a world that has suffered terribly from the horror of war…and rebellion. As a lad, I felt that there was no way possible to live a life where peace reigned supreme.

Bombs were being dropped all over the world, which led to more bombs being dropped. However, that "tit for tat" practice did not seem to work. Finally, after much suffering and destruction, PEACE was declared. Random acts of kindness took the place of death and destruction.

A young soldier, on Occupation duty, in what had been Enemy Territory, lived with people who'd been under foreign rule, but were now at peace.

They showed kindness to this young island lad very far from home, much to his gratitude and relief.

######

THE LAST TREE STANDING IN THE FOREST

By David Barwise

Last week, my wife and I were invited to attend the celebration of a family we had worked with some forty years before.

It was easy to recognize the parents who looked much the same as they did when we saw them last. The father may have had less hair on his head and the mother was less talkative, but it was the children who were like strangers to us. They had GROWN UP!

I felt like a tree that had feelings, standing alone in a forest of strangers. Most of the people there knew us, but we did not know many of them as the years had turned the children we'd known into adults.

"And he shall be like a tree planted by the rivers of water, that bringeth forth His fruit in his season…" as Psalm One says.

Life becomes different for us as the days and years roll on. We are, of course, called to live 'one day at a time,' and to accept the change each day brings.

######

THE LETTER

By David Barwise

I was born on a farm and grew up as a lad during the period known as The Great Depression. Mother and Father had spent all the money they had to buy that farm but times were very hard, so they were unable to make the payments necessary to become its owners.

My parents lost the farm and had to move into a deserted house several miles away. There was a blacksmith shop there where Grandfather (Dad's father) made his living, shoeing horses and repairing farm machinery.

The letter I write today is for my parents and in it, I wish to express my gratitude for enabling us to survive during difficult years.

Dear Mother and Father,

I want to thank you for doing everything you could, making it possible for my sisters and I to grow up and live happy lives during the Depression years.

I am sure that, when you married, you planned for lives of happiness for yourselves and your children. Happiness was not lost, but it was experienced in the midst of tremendous hardship.

The love you showed to us children, of whom I am one, made it possible for all of us to survive.

Thank you for your love, guidance and support during all the years we were together.

Your Son,
David

######

A PRISONER'S DELIGHT

By Gale Marks

It was fun visiting five days over Thanksgiving with my family in Minnesota. Well, except for the newest member: an eager, 7-month-old, oversized Lab puppy! She was confined to the kitchen by baby gates. However, we humans spent most of our time there in that very room. It meant that this senior member of the family was challenged to climb over the gate to enter and be greeted by the leaping, barking animal every time, without ever falling down.

In the beginning I returned the greeting with *hellos* and pats on the bobbing head. By the last day, I was shouting "NO" which drew a satisfactory response from the dog but hurt feelings from my son, who said, "She's only a puppy being herself."

I felt like saying, "I'm only a grandmother being herself," but decided not to.

The good part was the animal required lots of doggie walks in the park across the street in which we all took part. There was always good conversation and the weather was atypical for November in Minnesota, sunny and mild. Marvelous!

Our Thanksgiving meal preparation is always a family collaboration, each member attending to his/her specialty. My grandson and I had thirds. Does that say it?

On Sunday, at the Minneapolis airport for the trip to Rhode Island, I had mixed feelings of sadness in leaving the family I love and pleasure in looking forward to some time-out. I boarded the plane and began looking for, fingers crossed, seat 13B. I found it.

Uh-Oh. My seatmates were a young mother and her 7-month-old baby boy. Here we go again.

The conscientious mother spoke up immediately saying the baby had been well behaved on the trip out and she hoped he wouldn't be too bothersome on the trip back. I told her he was a beautiful baby and don't worry about it.

We laughed that our families had had reverse parallel experiences. I lived in Rhode island and our son had attended Earlham College in Indiana, met a mid-western girl, married her and has lived in Minnesota ever since. My seatmate, Minette, grew up in Minnesota and attended Brown University, met her future husband there and has settled in Rhode Island. She was coming home from visiting her parents and I was coming home from visiting my son.

Now Minette was concentrating on getting her baby to sleep and I was reading my book. All was well until I noticed that Minette was vomiting into a plastic bag that she held in one hand while she clasped the baby in the other.

"How can I help"? She shook her head.

"Want me to take the baby"?

"Yes," she moaned, "his name is Patrick."

Done. The poor girl finally finished.

"If you want to go to the Ladies Room, we'll be fine," I said.

She nodded, saying, "Patrick likes motion and music."

"Got it," I said, baby and I getting out of our seats while she followed.

Patrick and I danced in the aisle and I sang, "Momma's got a tummy ache and she'll be back in a moment. Momma's got a ..."

Minette returned with a smile on her face.

We resettled ourselves and I could see the stewardess rolling her cart up the aisle.

"Minette, the stewardess is coming and I'm getting a ginger ale. You want one, too? It might settle your stomach. We can put it on my tray table."

She asked for a glass of hot water to put Patrick's bottle in, too.

Bottle heated, milk gulped, baby asleep, Mom with head

back, eyes closed and I reading my book. All was quiet from then on.

When we landed, I offered to carry her bag as I did not have a carry-on. Minette nodded and said, "I can't thank you enough for all the help you've given us."

"It was a treat to be able to," said I.

Her husband was waiting at the bottom of the escalator. I handed him the suitcase and said, "What a great baby you have and your wife's not bad either."

He said, "Yeah, I got a good one."

I went off to claim my bag and felt like yelling, "Hi Ho Silver, away!" And of course they would be asking, "Who was that masked lady?"

######

1953 — THE YOUNG COUPLE

By Gale Marks

We finally got a house of our own. One of the best parts is, now we can have a dog. We bought a black Cocker Spaniel and named him, Tony.

Barry and I were the only couple in this close neighborhood without children. Pretty soon I was walking around the block in maternity clothes. Different neighbors stopped me to make pleasant remarks about my "expecting." But Helen was the last to speak up even though she was my next-door neighbor. She had a young son named Tommy.

One day Helen approached me and said, "You won't believe what Tommy just asked me."

"Oh," I said, "about this?" and I point to my tummy.

She said, "Yes. He asked me, do you think Mrs. Marks is going to have another Cocker Spaniel?"

"Oh no," said I. "What did you tell him?"

"I said, I don't know. We'll just have to wait and see."

"You didn't!"

"No, not really. But you do spend a lot of time with your dog."

Instead, it turned out to be our son, Stephen Alan Marks.

A full-time job, at last!

######

THESE ARE A FEW OF MY FAVORITE THINGS

By Gale Marks

THAT MAKE ME SMILE ...

...It has been a dark, overcast day. Just as I feel the need for some exercise and fresh air, the sun appears,

...I'm driving on the highway after too late a start and ahead of me, I can see the traffic light is red. Just as I approach, it turns green,

...It's 12:30, time for lunch. I open the refrigerator door and see there is one more serving left of Belmont's seafood salad,

...When I walk past the top of my neighbor's driveway I can see Ben and Jerry wagging their fannies and their tails while barking up a storm. They are hoping for a visit from me and know that I have dog biscuits in my pocket. Should I stop to visit, they will politely sit for the biscuit, then Jerry uses the length of his long tongue and gives me a very full swipe across the face as a *thank you* kiss. It takes a while before I can smile,

...I walk out to the mailbox in front of my house and besides the seven requests for donations I find a happy letter from one of my kids,

...The girl my son picked to be my daughter-in-law.

######

MY DEAREST CLAUDIA

By Davis Fogg

My Dearest Claudia,

I am so grateful that your construction is finished. Frankly the noise was getting to me.

The plumbing and electrical work wasn't so bad. A couple of trucks parked in the driveway for two weeks were tolerable, but annoying, as I had to park my car on the street. It was sideswiped by your painter's van but Crotty's Body Shop did a fine job of making it right. My insurance company deducted an additional $500 from the payout, as I hadn't read the "stupid parking exclusion" in my policy.

The plumbing was not one of your stellar moments. The water from the flood in the condo's basement was six inches deep, but filled with young bass. It was enough to soak my tax records, photographs, and wick up on my winter clothes. It's summer, so I won't worry about it now. That the electricity was out for five days while we were away, was a bit of a mess. The shrimp and fish in the freezer smelled like hell. I thought someone had died. And I shelled out another $500 to replace the stuff.

I did resent your tearing out and replacing the plaster walls. In my view, the old walls were just fine. The screech and explosive cracks of ripping out the framing, the ever present whine and grind of the buzz saw, and the bam-bam-bam of the stud drivers necessitated that I move into the Holiday Inn until you were finished. An awful place! I still have a headache from the first onslaught. You know, of course, that some errant workmen, upon entering or leaving the building, scraped dirt and plaster off their feet onto my valuable oriental carpet, ignoring the utilitarian mat that I placed in the hall for that purpose.

Need I mention again, the trampling of my annuals bed in the circle in front of the entrance, and the paint solvent poured over the boxwoods in front? At least you could have had the damn, gasping things drizzled green instead of purple. And painting the screen between our patio an electric pink, with those little purple Las Vegas sparkles in the paint, was a bit much. What was wrong with the old and proven green?

You've dragged this out for better than a year. Fevered activity punctuated by long intervals of relative silence while I waited for the other shoe to drop. That idiot, grumpy handyman George, comes in almost every day, and takes all day to pound a handful of nails in the wall next to our bedroom—usually during my morning and afternoon naps. I really think that George is fundamentally a nice fellow and don't blame him as he is taking orders from you. But he takes all afternoon to bang in a handful of nails. The smell of pot is nice though. He gave me a few sticks the other day. This has turned into one of the rare positives about your renovation. Instead of my taking a nap, we sit on the back stoop, pass as joint, get giggly and talk about how weird you are.

I must say that the worst thing is that yippy, whining, overindulged, mange and flea-ridden terrier of yours. Barks all the time and poops on the front door stoop. It took half an hour to clean my shoes yesterday. They still smell. Dog bit me on the leg last week as I was carrying in groceries. I bit him back.

Finally, though, I am very grateful to you for, at last, stopping all the noise. So suddenly and unexpectedly. The silence is platinum with diamonds. I'm also happy that this letter will never be sent.

Thank you for answering my heartfelt prayers and dying last week.

Sincerely yours,

Dave

8 June 2014

######

COME DANCE WITH ME

By C. Davis Fogg

You see, we'd never discussed marriage. Not a breath was wasted on it. It was an unspoken taboo. She told me right from the beginning of our two-year sometimes blissful, sometimes tumultuous relationship, that she would never marry again. Two were enough. She walked out of both of them. Without notice—just walked. Too confining she said. This was very scary to me. She liked to take off at a moments notice to some strange port or land, with a girlfriend, or a boy friend for all I knew, and wander back when she choose. I knew she would come back to me sometime. But she wanted untrammeled freedom. She would swim naked at a public beach, cavort like Zelda in the fountain in front of the Plaza, and dance braless on the bar at the village biker hangout, Hog Heaven.

But I was ready to tie the knot. I didn't want this woman that I love, in the most unbounded mystical, spiritual and witnessed way—an announcement to the world that we were together. Mine! Hands off. The question was how to convince her to say yes. Tell her that I would deliver riches and perpetual bliss? Maybe she would buy into nesting. We weren't exactly young chicks. Sooner or later all the free eagles do, why not us?

I figured I'd float a poem and a ring, and see if she'd take the bait. The question was where would I land the "will you marry me" punch line.

I pondered my options:

- Get down on my knees at "One if by Land; Two if by Sea" down in the village—arguably the most romantic restaurant in New York?
- Rent a plane to fly around a glittering Manhattan at night, read the poem and rely on the magic of the sparkling city to inspire her to agree?
- Take her to Vegas; get her a little drunk, and do the three-minute service at the Elvis Magnificent Marriage Mill?

None of these seemed quite right, the latter two a real hassle. So I went with my gut. When she arrived on a flight from LA one night, I surprised her by picking her up in a sparkling white stretch limo. She greeted me with the widest, warmest smile, succulent lips and closest body press I'd ever had. She was soooo happy to see me. I knew the time was right. So I read my poem as we went over the 59th Street Bridge toward home. It went like this:

Kate sweet Kate
Come dance with me
To billowing isles and azure seas
A million colors ply the deep
A million secrets there to keep

Fragrant eves romance and love
Nature, freedom, lust above
Laughter, jokes, intimacies shared
Freely given, freely bared

Your lips that taste my finger's trace
Your nose, your nape, your back, your breasts
Sleepy bodies rolling with soft swells
Close, tenderly, feeling well

Our trance, lost innocence in passion locked
Pounding abandon, tender rock
A fleeing moment in infinite time
A starry memory, just yours and mine.

So Kate sweet Kate
Please marry me

And dance with me
Through eternity

"til the end of time
'til the end of time

Be Mine

As he bridge lights strobed quickly by the car, she said without hesitation: Yes, Yes, Yes. I'll love you 'til the end of time.

26 April 2014

######

THE THIN RED LINE

By C. Davis Fogg

They call it the Thin Red Line now. But that's the name of a novel describing the event. Its real name was Lunga Ridge. Marines call it "bloody ridge" for, indeed, it soaked up the blood of 1000 brave men on both sides of the line. It was 1000 yards of a high, narrow, jungle-walled ridge that paralleled the Lunga river. It was also site of the battle that turned the tide of the Guadalcanal invasion in our favor. Some say that it put the Japanese on the defensive for the rest of the war, as they later abandoned the Island damaged, depleted, and ignominiously defeated.

I lost my buddy Louie Vestiano that night. It was his first and last time in combat. His only enemy to this point, aside from training targets, was the malaria-drenched and fetid jungle. His head was split open by a Jap bullet during their first charge on our position on top of the narrow spine of the ridge. There was a splintering crack, the whoosh of Vestiao's last breath as he fell, and his brains and blood spattered all over my face, hands and uniform. I was sick; then madder than hell. I became a vengeful focused bloodthirsty warrior. An adrenaline crazed monster. The night was so black and the smoke so thick that you could barely see the Japs running up the ridge, bayonets fixed, machine guns rattling behind them in support. The ghostly wraiths spewed pinpoints of yellow light reminding me of flocks of blinking fireflies on a lazy summer evening at home. I got my first Jap when he lunged over the ridge, bayonet out front. I had the advantage; I lay lower than him and stabbed him in the gut as he came over. He was groaning, covered in blood, and repeatedly crying out for someone in his strange sing-song voice. He took a long time to die. After the fight was over, I looked at what he had in the pockets of his tunic. There was a packet of letters from home, an unfinished letter, and a sepia- toned picture of him with a beautiful young wife and-two children—girl, maybe five, and a younger boy. I put the items back, save his miniature battle flag, and moved on.

Louie was practically the company's mascot. A short little black-haired Italian kid, he was only 18, and from Boston's North End. He had come straight from Camp Lejeune by way of a vomitus ten-day troop ship ride to the Solomons. He had a ready wink and smile and was exactly the kind of kid you'd like for your best friend in High School. He was always joking or playing practical jokes on his comrades. And, when camped, always had a cigar clamped between his teeth. It seems that a box of the Colonel's treasured cigars and a bottle of scotch, had been replaced by rolls of rough, ready, sandpapery, olive drab toilet paper. We had hundreds of thousands of marines worldwide in this war and it always amused me to think of how many freighters full of TP it took to keep the guys supplied. The Colonel was furious and went on a witch-hunt to recover the loot, but no one snitched, and Louie continued to preen with his cigars.

Some fifty years later, I'm standing on the well-worn dirt path of the ridge now, with my feet on either side of the thin red line. I am alone. Few visit this remote ridge on this insignificant island one thousand miles from anything else in the swallowing, deep blue Pacific. At the end of the path there is a modest gazebo-like marble monument to the some 1000 American and Japanese soldiers that died that night.

The late afternoon sun spills its warmth on the dense and variegated green carpet of trees painting the distant, high mountains. Storybook cumulous clouds float on a bright blue sky. A wisp of smoke trickles from a village here and there. The occasional Macaw heaves a raucous call to a mate. The usual blast furnace temperature is kept at bay by a gentle, sweet, unseasonably cool breeze swelling up from the invasion beach. The verdant scene covers the bones and souls of the soldiers who died there; the corpses of airplanes and guns and the graveyard of thousands of dreams.

I still hate the Japs, but not so much now as then. They were drafted kids too, and just as terrorized as we.

22 May 2014

######

But, God—Two Worlds Collide

By Dawn Paoletta

I grew up with a very bad perspective about marriage. I witnessed firsthand the worst aspects of it, instead of the beautiful gift it potentially can be for people. My husband, on the other hand, has a Catholic background and a stronger positive impression of marriage than I. This is thanks to the sweet example of his parents who have been married for 54 years. Our backgrounds are as different as night and day. Consider that God did marry the night and day after all in Genesis, now that I think of it. A creative matchmaker He is, I would dare say.

It is July 1983. I am working at a little Salad/Yogurt place in Downtown Providence called Natural Sweetness. I am in the role of Supervisor at 18 years old. He begins work after school, 16. I am his boss.

See me smiling. See God beginning His amusing work and knitting destiny, unknowingly for us. I am getting back on track after a young life of, for lack of a better word, rebellion. Which at this point, really is not finished. His mom works across the street at Blue Cross and has landed him an after school job by inquiring of the Manager.

He comes in and I hand him one of my infamous "To Do" lists. I am obsessed with keeping the upstairs well stocked. He lugs bottles, jugs, jars and boxes up and down the stairs. It is my job to train him. Train him I do. I hand him the mop. I close out the register. He quietly works. At the end of our shift he takes a bus home. I take a bus to the other side of the city.

I am not sure at what point we become friends. I observe him. Young, hard working. I feel old. Well beyond my years. I feel somewhat protective of him and yet, I myself am in need of protection. I am crass to his class, and we do become friends, eventually. What it means at the time is not what either of us expects.

The beginning of our friendship will be the start of a commitment of a lifetime. But at this point in time he is in school and I am travelling a road to nowhere. But God, my friends, is in it. Right from the start. Isn't He always?

If anyone would have said to me right then, this is your future husband, I would have thought they were crazy. I was not figuring him anymore than God because at this point God was as distant to me as the possibility of marrying him. Or anyone. But, God.

######

If I Never (A Million Twists of Fate)
by Dawn Paoletta

If I had never been online,
Never watched "You've Got Mail",
   Considered it good to talk to strangers.

If I had never drove into that house,
With my red Javelin,
Or tried to please everyone else,
   By compromising myself.

If I had never chosen cash,
Over a memory,
Traded that which never stays
For that which can never be regained.

If I had never opened the door
To danger when it came knocking
Dressed in desperation —
But then again,
I've always been a sucker for a bleeding heart,
Especially when combined with danger and
desperation.

If I had never succumbed to temptation,
For the umpteenth time
Well, I guess I wouldn't be human,
So scratch that premise completely.

If I'd never
Been his boss,
His friend,
His love, his wife
Never seen the providence of god
Or longed for the cobblestone streets of Nantucket

If I never brought tears to my mother's cheeks
While sharing news,

In the kitchen.
Or been reborn, or led astray, or ran away,
or met the dawn
Boldly —
Fearlessly,
Forsaking sleep
If I'd never chased the moon on a starlit night,
Just because…
Life is short,
And sunrise is better than sunset
And the beginning, always better than the end
Living, better than dying,
Hello better than goodbye

And perhaps,
as the good professor told me
On that walk in the Berkshires
That it is the journey,
the seeking itself,
Not the end, that is significant.

After many years of pondering,
 I might like to go back in time to our walk and
conversation,
inform him,
I do believe,
he is misinformed —
Indubitably wrong...

Not the journey, not the end,
But all the glory
Is in the beginning,
Inevitably, and always.
Again and again.

######

MY SECRET STRENGTH
By Dawn Paoletta

Untangle my messy mind
clear my head and thinking
Immerse me in your word
that I may surely find...

Is it so wrong to long for a normal day?
What need then would I have to pray?
I could argue, still, I'd give thanks and pray...

Instead I see
to grow nearer to thee
is to praise and thank on bended knee—
right here in this current adversity.

For you are my secret strength
I hide in the shadow of your wing
waiting for the storm to calm
for hope your love does bring

In the meantime
I'll raise my voice
claiming your name
above the noise

In my closet
I will bow down
whispering prayers of grace
awaiting your blessed arrival
and to gaze upon your glorious face.

For now I lay in wait
holding firm thy sharpened sword
Relying on Your Spirit—
mighty power of the Lord.

######

FEELINGS

By Dawn Paoletta

Where do feelings come from?
Where do they go?
Who do they run to?
Why do they show?

Feelings, Feelings,
 I've had my share
But the greatest feeling of all
comes with a dare

Listen closely, darlings
if you really care

What is the greatest of all
feeling I have had
I'm getting pretty old,
my memory is bad

Can I single out
one monumental event
an emotional climax
from heaven sent

I think not.

Life allows so many
 emotional displays
yet the greatest
is the one that leads me away

Away to where, you might say.

I'll tell you now
Hang on and stay...

Mastering all
that I fear
by confronting each
 face first

and those things that lead to selflessness

for these I do thirst

Unseen deeds, that encourage others and
allow me to forget
my own personal woes, trials and debt.

I dare you, I dare you
to seek these things:

Selflessness, Fearlessness—
True freedom each brings!

#####

THE DISTRACTED WRITER
By Dawn Paoletta

The teacher with her singsong voice
shares the writing prompt
which sets my mind a spinning
not unlike a top

ideas shoot out like sparks from my brain
and I begin to write
But then a fire starts
just within my sight

I pause to tend this current distraction
deal with it swiftly
I get back to this call to action

I sit again, pen in hand
awaiting sparks to fly
then, lo and behold
right before my eye

A bird through the window
—such a glorious sight!
I must get a closer look
in the clearer light

Now wait a minute
where was I
and just what was I doing?

Writing, writing, ah -ha,
That's it!
my mind begins a stewing

Now focus, stay with it,
grab paper and pen
Just sit already,
be still—
Here we go again!

######

DAILY RX FOR GRACE
By Dawn Paoletta

Arise! Awake refreshed to the dawn.
Begin each day as one seeing for the first time
Consider your time carefully, with whom and how you will
spend it,
Delighting in all that is, and is not.
Embrace each moment as a gift, for you know not when the
party ends.
Forget the pain of the past,
Give your heart over to beauty-it will surely restore your
soul's joy-
Hold back nothing, whether passion, graciousness, or love
Inspire others along the path as you travel, you know not
whether your paths will cross again,
serendipitously.
Journey not always alone, but offer
Kindness to stragglers and those on the fringe.
Leave behind all that hinders you or clutters your clarity, but
Make room for spontaneous surprises, strangers and sages.
Nothing in life is purposeless.
Overlook small offenses, perhaps even a few big ones; it'll
boggle minds, wake a soul up.
Punctuate all with enthusiasm, and a smile whenever the
circumstance invites-but also when it doesn't;
It'll surely drop some jaws, and close a few others.
Quietly offer encouragement if it is within your power,
Remembering many carry burdens unknown, unseen.
Start a revival of kindness, because despite what the world
says, Nice really does matter...
Trust that it can save lives because it can and does.
Unanimously agree with yourself, and you will be ahead of
the game; treat yourself like your own
greatest love, or best friend. If no one else believes in you,
YOU believe in you. Who has time for arguing
with that logic?

######

HATE IS NOT IN MY VOCABULARY ANYMORE

By Cheryl Voisinet

I wrote that

I was in love

with everything

with life

It came to me in a dream

I could not deny its power

After all – it was the strength

I needed

######

THE RIVER

By Cheryl Voisinet

I remember the summer

when the wood porch felt warm

under my bare feet

The aroma of quahogs

we dug from the sea floor

mingles with the scent of sweet sausage

Red, white and blue bud cans cracking,

Quenching that first ice cold sip

On this porch under a grape leaf canopy

I sit lazy and satisfied

Boaters waving, children squealing,

Black lab barking, ginger cat running

This river love affair began many

Summers ago with Mississippi misadventures

Of boys named Tom and Huck

Feeling the water, soft through my fingers

I laughed and swam across the currents

A Pisces dream of sun sparkled reflections

Enough to bring tears to my eyes

######

VALENTINE'S DAY

BY Cheryl Voisinet

A red plastic heart awaits

on a white frosted cupcake

on this 14th day of February 730 days ago.

Friends have left;

we are alone …*Marry me.*

I remind him we are already:

when we drank moonshine by the bonfire

at Christmas and

your buddy announced:

I am a Justice of the peace.

But we were reckless in our response.

We did not see ourselves behind the masks

forever in the future,

forever in the past.

Our synthetic feelings covered in cheese and ketchup.

If I wanted crumbs, I'd be a bird

If I wanted carrots, I'd be a rabbit.

6 March 2014

######

ACTS OF KINDNESS ARE CARRIED IN HEARTS

By Marty Decker

Kindness is stored in depths of one's heart.
Included in self, not set apart.
It is evident in one's bearing,
Always available for sharing.
The giver's act is so spontaneous,
Ending with a treasure so glorious.
Bequeathed because it has to be done,
Acts of kindness become such great fun.
Kind people live among all of us
Acting so good, without any fuss.

######

Escaping the MRI
By Marty Decker

The doctor ordered me to have an MRI to take a look at my shoulder. The range of motion was severely limited. I could not throw a soft ball or raise the arm sideways without severe pain. The Medico suspected that there were severe bone spurs.

I reported to the MRI technician, who instructed me to lie quietly without moving during the picture taking. She estimated I would be in the machine about twenty minutes at the most. Then she helped me slip into the machine. She turned it on. It was noisy with its continuous clicking. The technician kept talking with me as pictures were taken. After about five minutes, she told me the process would take longer, maybe even forty-five minutes.

I am more than a tad claustrophobic, so the thought of remaining immobilized forty minutes more while being clicked at without cessation was unnerving. I found a way to escape: I envisioned playing string bass, on which I was then playing. In my imagination, I started focusing on the F—major scale, carefully placing my fingers to get the right tone and stroking the bow to bring out a round and even tone. I named each note as I played to make sure I was playing the scale properly.

I played slowly and repeated each at least twice, so I could stay occupied with the playing for as long as possible. When I tired of the scales, I switched to etude number eight, from Franz Simandl's book, and then "The Elephant" from "Parade of the Animals" by Camille Saint Saens' "Carnival of the Animals".

The imaged activity seemed very real. I heard the notes, felt the muscular tensions and experienced the feeling of arm and finger movements. Time passed, I felt only the pleasure of playing and reliving the praise I received for producing 'real music' at my recital. I slid out of that infernally tight space gladly, still in my usual, almost sane, state of mind.

Unfortunately, bone spurs were indeed a problem and surgery was necessary. I was anaesthetized for that and did not have to imagine anything.

######

PEOPLE AND ME

By Marty Decker

I come most alive when I interact face-to-face with others, but being alone is not necessarily depressing. I use several actions to keep my mood elevated.

Memories of music associated with upbeat times spent with others is especially uplifting. Hearing the Glen Miller military march version of W.C. Handy's St. Louis Woman lifts me sky high. I am sent to nirvana by the music, the sunlit scenes of an October day on a football field, and the wildly provocative posturing of an incredibly statuesque blond drum majorette who guides our band as we dance across the field.

Visions of the mezzo soprano solos from the Messiah, sung by my new girl Martha, came to transport me to the wonders of her voice and times together as I drove her to and from the rehearsals and listened to her sing during college Christmas break. The sound of her singing "Every Valley" and "He Shall Feed His Flock" still brings semi-ecstasy.

When I do my workouts, playing CD's fills my head with images and thoughts of music in joyous settings. Hearing the voices and seeing those images fills me with the goodness of being alive.

Even at times of lonely stress, I can use images of scale exercises and etudes from past music study to occupy my thoughts, banishing the blahs and creating the aaahs.

At sleeping time when my mind is heavy, the memories of song and setting relax me and put me at an ease that leads to sleep. The musical sounds, images of people and prized settings lead me to the top of the world.

######

RR COMMUTING TO NY CITY
By Marty Decker

Conversations are the buttered popcorn of traveling, giving stuff to chew that is tasty and entertaining, maybe even a bit nourishing.

"Is this seat taken; okay if I sit here?"

"It belongs to you! Are you going to Hartford?"

"No, just to Meriden. I go back and forth on Tuesday and Friday."

"I'm going to New Britain. I go into the City three days a week – on the through train from Montreal in the morning, then this one back home in the afternoon."

"That's a long day! I stay in town. I dance with the June Taylor Dancer's on the Jackie Gleason Show and help my husband run a dance school in Meriden. What do you do?"

"I'm a psychologist at Trinity College. I'm on sabbatical spending the year with a group studying competency based teaching at City University. I organize and manage workshops for City University faculty members. I live in Newington with my wife and three kids.

"Riding Amtrak is great. It's a really civilized way to travel isn't it? You can relax, get something to eat, and even do some work."

"That's true.' I'm able to read five or six books a week. The student librarian claims the only one who reads more than me is God!

"It's much more relaxing than driving or even taking bus. There's room to move around; go to a dining car to eat and drink, seats are comfortable and the cast changes daily."

"I'll point you out to my kids when I watch Jackie Gleason, Sunday. That'll impress them."

" I hope it works. We'll probably see each other again on a Friday night.

######

A Conversation At Camden, Maine

By Stephen Hiss

"Afternoon, Ira."

"Hello Jake."

"Did you leave early, Ira?"

"Yea, getting' too old to be luggin' those traps off them lobsta boats, 'specially in this cold and snow bein' over ma ankles."

"I doun know, why they can't clear some of that snow so we can work betta."

"You do know why Jake. It's 'cause they know we'll work in it any way."

"Every year the same thing...and they know it."

"Yea, Jake, I know. Sometimes I sit in this old haaba café and wonda bout how things changed from when we did real work on boats."

"I know, Jake, those days are long gone. I think 'bout those old times and 'member how good it felt to see them schooners comin' in and needin' fixin' done—some of 'em all broken up and expectin' us to put 'em back together in no time a'tall."

"Yea, I member that tough ass yardsman watchin' and yellin' at me, Ira!... '"Be sure you're shavin' those Ash boards right, and make sure they're trimmed so they'd fit good into that crown moldin' at that ball.'

"That was my special job and he made sure I did it right. He was a ornery cuss, but Jake, he knew how to fix wood boats and could take on jobs on those old boats as good or better than any of us."

"Ira, your right sure 'bout that... can't deny any of it...I'm lookin' at those rail tracks ova there...Jake... leadin' from the water 50 feet or so into Emil's ole boat barn, and it brings back more memories."

"I can still see Emil standin' inside hutched back a little on his heels and pullin' on his beard as those old boats bein' wenched' along those rails and into his barn."

"I remember that too, Ira...he'd be watchin' a boat comin' in and before it got tied to the bulkhead in that barn Emil would have seen most times what the problem was and already figured out how to make it right again."

"You know, Ira, I could see him in that barn sometimes one 'n two in the mornin' workin' so the lobstamen could be out fishin' again in a day or two."

"He'd have so many laterns lit in that barn so he could see what he was doin'...that if you didn't know better...you'd think the whole place was on fire."

"Yea, those were good days...but ya know, some things are still the same."

"What do ya mean Ira?"

"Well, look at that island standing proud right in the middle of ole' Camden Harbor makin' every yachtman and fisherman watch out for 'em on their way in...it ain't moved an inch for anybody for thousan's a years."

"And look't those mountains and rocky cliffs comin' right down to the water with their trees all bend over from the snow weighin' them down."

"They ain't changed a'tall...year after year... they're right there."

"Yea... but that's only cause nobody can get at 'em."

"There is one old shipwright who's still workin' the old way down in Rockport."

"Yea, Sam...who is that?"

"It's ole man Vespa. He come over from Italy 40 years ago—a simple yard worker usin' what he learned at his old yard back home...and today he's somebody who the toughest trust to work on their wooden boats."

"Well, maybe you're right. Not everything is changed and gone, and I'm wishin' him the best and to keep on doin' it."

Well, Ira, I gotta' go. It's getting' late and Mary probably has suppa ready for the table."

"Ok Jake, see ya at six tomorra' mornin' so we can pull those traps from Nathan's boat."

"Good night."

"Yep..."

######
— 91 —

A THANK YOU LETTER

By Stephen Hiss

Dear Mom and Dad,

I've been asked to write a letter of thanks to someone who has had an important impact on my life. It's a difficult assignment because when I think about all the many things various people have done for me, along with their individual efforts I realize volume doesn't necessary count. Who I am today is simply an accumulation of all those things I have been given and experienced throughout my life with the both of you and others. My strong tendency to analyze leads me to think a little self-assessment may be in order because without an honest and accurate accounting of self, it's hard for me to understand for what and to whom I should be most thankful.

I've been fortunate in many ways. Even during those times when the emotional and economical well-being of our family had been tested and threatened, I had enough food, clothing, and emotional support. Sometimes I hear hear people talk about those years being the "good old days." But I remember those as the times our family and many around us experienced the greatest challenges and threats. I began to realize those good old days were not so good after all and the only reason people can look back fondly is simply because they were able to find ways to get through OK, and today have the advantage and comfort of knowing it all worked out and they are safe. I am very thankful for your guidance and all that you both struggled to provide our family during those times. The many examples of how mental and internal toughness can be balanced with kindness and gentleness have never left me. Not only during those times, but also throughout my life, those qualities have manifested in countless sacrifices for me.

But it's not the number of things people do, it's the whats and hows, and for me while trying to be as honest with myself as possible, I realize the most important gift you both gave me is the heart to be generous, the strength in self to be fair-minded, and the intellect and expanding wisdom to appreciate the value of life's lessons and strength to press forward with my convictions. In short you have given me a good life, so how can I possibly thank you?

Once again I found the answer in a conversation I had with Mom a long time ago. Her answer has become a lifelong journey I have yet to complete. She simply said the best way to thank me, "is to do for Kimberly and Laura what we have done for you."

Your loving son,

Steve

######

THE MAN AT THE TABLE

By Stephen Hiss

It was lunchtime and while taking a short walk on the Atlantic City boardwalk, I decided to stop in to see the newest casino. As I walked in, and seeing all the glitz and noise around me, I noticed a tattered looking man at a table. I'm guessing he's been on the planet for about 75 years. He didn't look weak, just thin and worn—tired. Standing there at the table he was tentative—thinking, anticipating, and maybe hoping. His hair is mostly grey, unkempt, and from the back he looked sad, which was in sharp contrast to lively music and laughter around him at the table. It's hard to guess at what he's thinking—but I was sure whatever it was wasn't good.

If he had a good life, he was on hard times then, or maybe he was always on hard times, an abstract. Someone who never quite got in with the rhythm of society, or maybe, he had been a pillar of society and the strength of his family but was dealt a life changing blow we hear about occasionally, and never recovered.

Below the sleeve of his sagging herringbone jacket his hand was holding chips and it twitches every moment or so as though he just had made his decision to get in the game— and then he pulled back, held, and watched for another few moments.

I wondered how many people with stories like his went through there every year. Risking a little or all to escape from who and where they were—or perhaps climb out from where they had been. How many actually succeed versus the numbers who didn't, and what happened to those who didn't. I don't know whether to feel sorry and have the deepest empathy for him or see him for being a fool as he made that bet, but I should be careful to make judgment—because what lay ahead for me tomorrow is also unknown.

######

PROMISES

By Stephen Hiss

Why make promises?

Many are broken or only partially fulfilled having little impact on the life of the intended beneficiary. In other instances, broken promises have altered lives of people in the worst possible way. Yet promises are made by virtually everyone—often, and about things that range from the sublime to the most meaningful. In fact, it seems we have become so conditioned to promises that upon receiving a promise, we almost immediately begin to hear a subtle and protective voice inside alerting us of a possible alternative or breach.

It seems most if not many promises aren't really promises at all. They are simply very good intentions that are stated in a particular way.

Actually, it is the action and the outcome that is the only promise that can be made, and the "word " a good feeling.

24 April 2014

######

THE MOST BEAUTIFUL ROSE
By Stephen Hiss

What was the happiest day of my life? Which rose of a bouquet of 12, 18, or even 24 is the most beautiful? Which has the most pleasing aroma? It's even more difficult when they are all different colors. Some showing a vibrant red, another crimson. One is a happy yellow. Still another a beautiful soft peach. Maybe it was our wedding day? No, it might be the morning of our first born, Kimberly. But I remember when our second born Laura came to us, maybe that was the happiest.

Well, wait a minute, perhaps it was the day I received my Masters Degree in Healthcare Administration after 25 continuous years of night school—or the day I saw my first book in print. Now let me think a little more about this. It could have been the morning after I took possession of my 30 foot sailboat and with great pride and trepidation began our maiden voyage very early one foggy Friday morning from southern New Jersey to Rhode Island with my oldest daughter, her friend, and a close family friend. I remember that exciting moment filled with wonder as we left the dock on that journey, and there would be others follow. Or that day I fulfilled a long held vision of sailing by the Statue of Liberty in New York Harbor—or was the last morning of that journey at 2:30AM while sailing in stormy weather I first spotted Beaver Light showing us the way.

Still, it could have been when Pat and I had our very first picnic dinner along the rocky shoreline in Jamestown as we watched huge waves crash and spray against the rocks on a beautiful evening and felt its spray blessing us. I remember that could have been the day… with the feeling I was finally home.

Someone asked Duke Ellington during an interview. "Of all the incredible music you wrote, which is your favorite?" As I watched, he smiled without pausing a second and said, "well …it's the next one I write."

Which of those roses is the most beautiful? Which of the colors makes me feel the happiest? I imagined and hoped for several of my happiest days, but never really believed they could happen. Sorry, I can't choose for as many different colors and scents there are in that bouquet, I think I'll take the Duke's lead and say, maybe my best—the happiest day is yet to come.

1 May 2014

######

THE PARADE

By Stephen Hiss

I see them coming just ahead,
around the turn
A few at first floating and spinning
three across, then four.
They come in waves,
Too many to count as they go by
Dancing and spinning to the music.

The music thunders in the distance
Then closer and distant again
The sound echoes continuously all around.

 I stand marveling at each performance
as the colors go by.
Brilliant yellows, reds, and even shinny greens
and as they come closer they begin to spin
as to anticipate the excitement from those who might
be watching
for their unique and special gestures.

Fall is a beautiful time of year for a parade.
The air is pleasant and dry.
The sky is crystal clear – deep blue in color
and the breeze has a quality that lets you know
the season is changing.

The entries float by and for another moment
the sound of the parade pulses with new excitement.
Here comes another entry spinning, gliding,
and twirling as the music punctuates the dancing.

As nature's music plays with its gentle rushes among
the trees,
they freely release their leaves and a new performance
begins,
and as they Fall the entire parade floats downstream.

I listen to nature's music in the trees,
The gurgling stream tumbling over rocks,
and I marvel at the magical spectacle
as fall's special parade floats by.

######

What Stirs Me

Stephen Hiss

I like taking pictures of nature, people, and things. I love sailing and trading great licks in a jazz solo with other musicians. And I enjoy writing. But what stirs me is not necessarily something tangible. What stirs and excites me comes from inside. It's my imagination and my thoughts that create an energy and sense of excitement, deep appreciation, amazement, and wonder. Those feelings and thoughts move me in ways I often can't explain. I wonder about how all the things around me fit together so beautifully on this earth.

How can the prevailing wind re-arrange molecules within a tree on the shore of Jamestown so that all of its branches grow hard to the northeast, or the feeling that takes over when biking on the boardwalk in Ocean City early in the morning and seeing the perfect symmetry of space and color as the ocean meets the sandy beach— which in turn works its way into high dunes that push against the boardwalk. How can moisture in the air work with gravity and thermal drafts to form clouds that resemble animals, mountain ranges and sometimes, even people. What about the excitement and relief I feel when reaching a harbor safely just before dark clouds form overhead and unleash lighting, rain, and wind. It's not the tree, the harbor, or those clouds—or even those abovementioned musical notes by themselves. No, what stirs me is the emotion, the anticipation, the wonder, and appreciation that gnaw and delight me all at the same time.

10 April 2014

######

WHY I WRITE
By Stephen Hiss

I'm most comfortable and more capable writing in a prose format. For me, writing is a kind of convenient catharsis. I say convenient because I can decide when and where to write and don't have to negotiate my thoughts through a conversation with another person, or a group. This is not to say I don't fully enjoy a good conversation, but when writing it's just me and my thoughts. Writing is a catharsis for me because it often triggers insights that seem to have been latent inside and waiting to be released. At times it has brought a more clear understanding of myself, things, and sometimes other people, which are all thoughts, ideas, and perspectives that probably would not have surfaced for me from another medium of expression.

Good writing should also be a trigger that evokes emotions, insights, and even new understanding discovered by the reader. Given that point of view, I believe the author assumes a kind of responsibility that goes beyond the mechanics of grammar and rules of good writing. I have come to see writing as a kind of seasoning for both the writer and the reader. As salt is absorbed by ingredients while cooking and releases new flavors in food, good writing allows the reader to absorb those new emotions and new thoughts from the author's words which then become part of the reader's new private and personal world. When writing, I enjoy exercising that challenge and that responsibility to the reader, because whether it be serious or simply for fun in doing so I gain the same for myself.

13 February 2014

######

A Child's Secret Hiding Place

By Monica Hickey May

Once upon a time there were two little sisters – Kathleen (8) and Monica (6) and we lived with our family in an old house in Scotland. We had a beautiful aunt – her name was Molly – and she came to visit us from the town of Glasgow.

One day she said that she had enrolled us in a very exclusive club – called the "Tinkerbells" and every week we would receive a set of instructions to enrich our lives – and $2.00 each to spend on anything we wanted.

Kathleen and I had dreamed of having enough money to buy Cadburys Chocolate Drops, a big favorite but I saw the value of making a secret reserve of sweets – while Kathleen couldn't resist all the temptation. She found that her $2.00 allowance was all used up and she had to wait for the next $2.00 to arrive from Glasgow!

Meanwhile, I saved up enough to open my own secret candy store. When the word got around that there were *Sweets for Sale* and that the payment was a small coin – I was ready to be open for business!!!

I learned at an early age the power of owning something that others wanted and their willingness to pay for it.

At 6 years of age, I became an entrepreneur.

Our brother, Terence was 8 years old and he was not invited because HE WAS A BOY – and spent hours training for the school's boxing matches.

######

WHAT IS YOUR FAVORITE ROOM IN THE HOUSE?

By Monica Hickey May

It only took me a minute to decide. In the corner of my living room there stands a bookcase – yes – many treasured books. I decided it was time to pay attention to the waiting shelves—many came with me from London (1953)—some borrowed and not yet returned—some books that belonged to Peter—art—dance—film—and, of course, it is fatal to start opening such wonderful books—histories of Russia—travel books from places visited—ad not visited!

Then those bridal history books—all about antique laces and laces from Belgium, reminding me of trips I took in search of wedding dresses—photographs for wedding planning—cakes by Sylvia Weinstock—flowers—music.

I am now ready to keep going—book by book—some to read again—"Angela Ashes"? For sure!

There's a tiny blue book—a gift to me from someone I loved and left when I left England.

Rupert Brooke, famed English poet who died in World War I—wrote, "If I should die, think only this of me—that there's some corner of a foreign field that is forever England." Rubert Brooke died in World War I and is buried in a foreign land.

Then, Robert Burns—a favorite Scottish poet of mine. He is immortalized forever—*"Should old acquaintance be forget and never brought to mind?*

Should old acquaintance be forgot and auld lang syne"?
(not a dry eye in the house).

Robert Burns was pursued by irate Scottish fathers who found their once-maiden daughters were with child—a missing poet—a wayward missing poet—but, once he died, all was forgiven and Burns was lauded and treasured as their own Scottish Poet.

But I digress—there's a new book—"A Thread of Grace" by Mary Doria Russell—all about how Italians worked to save and hide Jews in World War II.

On a tombstone in Italy these words are inscribed, "What you are, we were; what we are, you shall be." Truer words were never spoken.

The hours go by and I turn my attention to the photographs telling the story of our lives and I decide it is time to bid them a fond farewell until another day dawns, and I go to my wonderful writing class.

######

To Be—Or Not To Be

By Monica Hickey May

When President Obama finally proclaimed that he was for same sex marriage - I thought back to an era long ago:

Oscar Wilde – charming, witty, brilliant - parodied the vacant, upper class Victorian lives.

Oscar was born to a brilliant woman, part of the Dublin literati. She would have preferred a daughter—but Oscar was kept captive until he was 8 years old! She dressed him in fancy girls' clothes—and he was never allowed to go out and play with those "rough Irish boys."

Oscar's mother engaged him with large doses of Literature and the poets of the day. Is it any wonder how educated he was. He went to Trinity College in Dublin, founded by Queen Elizabeth I. He was known as a great wit— charming, a devastating observer of upper class hypocrisy. He was invited to all the soirees where he surely developed his writing skills...and then...to London society and his homosexual relationship with (Lord Alfred) Douglas—also from a prominent family—whose father, (the Marquess of Queensberry), made sure to destroy Oscar.

Oscar Wilde was imprisoned, which did not prevent him from writing "The Ballad of Reading Gaol."

It's 2014—years and years after Oscar Wilde's "crime" and punishment.

Would Oscar Wilde ever imagine that the President of the United States would take his final step on the road to same sex marriage?

As those outside the court railed against Obama's decision – and all the voices that are for and against the moving trend that may not be denied.

As Bob Dylan wrote, "The times, they are a-changing."

######

A LETTER TO MY DAUGHTER AT EASTER

By Monica Hickey May

Dear Caitlin—

You arrived with a lovely little Easter Basket—all lit up—to tell me,

"Yes, it's Easter Sunday."

Immersed in my New York Times—too much to read—too much to go out in the sunshine!

But you saw my outfit laid out on my bed—and said, "Let's go"— no destination until you said "SPAIN Restaurant"—a cast of thousands in fancy Easter outfits—the children with their IPods—the parents—the grandparents still there—and then EASTER!

It's Rhode Island shepherding their flock after Easter Sunday Mass. We sit at the bar and wait to hear the call "table for two."

Happiness together is bestowed on us—wonderful service—fabulous food—and a handsome young waiter who brings a tray of sweets to tempt us .

—Yes—Why not!!

Caitlin, you are a wonderful daughter, who brings light and joy not only for the Easter Bunny Basket.

Love,

Mother, Monica

######

DANCER'S WORLD

A Painting by my Late Husband –
Peter Glushanok   (40 x 46)

By Monica Hickey May

The stage is set—the cliffs meet the shimmering warm waves—inviting, coaxing the young dancers to dive in to the cooling waters. And, because the young have no fear, they dive in and the force of the undercurrent takes them down, down— and there they wait for the other dancers who would join them in an ecstasy of belonging to each other.

But they do not seem to find them as they search the deep blue sea! Down, down, down they dive until they reach the floor of the sea.

And then, to their horror – there to meet all of them—is the Monster Sea Serpent – who has reigned there forever.

He promises to make their acquaintance one by one.

######

Once Upon A New York Cat

By Monica Hickey May

It was November 2004 and I was about to leave New York City where I had lived since 1953 after emigrating from London, England and after surviving the war years.

It was hard to leave New York City and soon to arrive in Wakefield, Rhode Island without Rufus, my Maine Coon Cat.

I would have liked to have him live with me in Shadow Farm, but Rufus had a mind of his own and we sometimes have to pay the price for protesting without a thought of the consequences.

Rufus decided that he wanted no part of the move to Rhode Island and he showed his displeasure by destroying the soft black leather sofa cushions by ripping them to shreds. To complete his displeasure, he peed nightly to emphasize his grand gestures!

Rufus slept on the window seat in my bedroom and it was time to say *Good Night.* I awoke with a start—Rufus had just taken a bite out of my leg!

I now knew that his end was near!

I coaxed Rufus into his carry-on bag and, binding up my deep wound, I took a taxi to the A.S.P.C.A. I looked at Rufus and said, "You have committed Domestic Violence."

I bid him a fond farewell, remembering the happier days we had shared together. I was in tears as I signed his *Death Warrant.* Then, I took a taxi to Lennox Hill Hospital where I received Tetanus shots.

I called my daughter, Caitlin, and told her what had happened.

Caitlin said, "You mean you put Rufus down"?

I said, "Yes," Rufus had committed Domestic Violence.

Her husband, Bryan, said, "I had better watch my step with this family."

######

Horoscope Of The Day

By Guida Cole Schmedinghoff

AQUARIUS: Mistakes are just one of the things you'll make — and such a minor number of them that it's hardly worth worrying about.

As he slouched behind the wheel of his muscle car and headed for the freeway entrance to downtown, Andrew "Andy" Gray repeated his morning's horoscope over and over in his mind. He entered smoothly onto the freeway, checked his mirror, and pulled into the fast lane. It was a beautiful day and a real pleasure to be behind the wheel of such a capable car and before he thought about it, he was hitting almost 75 mph on his speedometer. He checked fore and aft, not a cop in sight, and hit the accelerator a second before the flashing light showed up in the mirror.

The officer was pleasant enough, gave him a ticket for doing 80 mph, a rehearsed talk about obeying those speed signs in the future, and took off.

Andy dropped that ticket in with the two (or was it 3?) he already had in the glove compartment. He found some music he liked on the radio, turned it up full blast, and proceeded down the highway, still feeling good about that horoscope this morning. He often had reservations about really believing in such things as horoscopes and fortune tellers, but his mother had just about convinced him they were for real. Keeping time with the music with his left hand on the steering wheel, he slowed for the exit marked "Utopia, 2 miles." He had never been to Utopia, didn't even know there was a town named Utopia, but, hey, this was a good day for him so why not go check it out? Who would name a town Utopia anyhow?

In order to turn right into the town, he had to go around a large clump of rhododendron bushes so he navigated carefully around them, straightened out on what appeared to be the main street of the town and there they were again: flashing lights in his rear view mirror. This time it was an apologetic looking little man who assured him there was, yes sir, there was a speed limit sign there, kind of hidden in the bushes, yes sir, they were going to have to clip back those bushes, the fine is fifty dollars sir, just pay me in cash and we will forget the ticket.

Andy knew a speed trap when he saw one, so he searched his wallet, fished out what appeared to be his last fifty dollars, bid the officer a good day, and went on his way.

He decided he had better fill the tank before he headed home, so he pulled into what looked like a large station with several tanks in evidence and plenty of lights. It also had plenty of customers, it turned out, and Andy had to pull his car behind a pick-up truck and take his place in a long slow-moving line of vehicles inching toward the pumps and a fill-up. He was sitting there in rather a fog when he heard, "Hey, you!"

He looked up to see a giant standing alongside his car. He seemed to be about the size of a tall Sumo wrestler as he leaned against the car, his large paw covering the side rear view mirror. In his other hand he held an open case to display a watch and, without any preliminary, he proceeded to hold this in front of Andy's face now while he asked, "How about a nice Rolex, feller? I can let you have it for only a hundred cash today if you don't ask too many questions, know what I mean?"

While he asked this, the giant had his hand busy just above the mirror. He would make a twisting motion with his hand over and over again, as though twisting the mirror and the chrome fitting attaching it to the car, right off and tossing it away, then making that motion over again so that the meaning was plain: buy a watch or lose a mirror.

Andy had had it. He didn't have $100 left anyhow, but he was tired of being played for a fool today and while he was telling his attacker that and just what he could do with that faux Rolex, he heard a terrible sound of tearing, crunching metal.

I have it on good authority that Andy cried that night for the first time since he was a small boy. He never read his horoscope again.

######

YESTERDAY AND TODAY

By Guida Cole Schmedinghoff

It's snowing again. This has been a terrible winter. I pull my down comforter up to my chin, fluff-up the pillows, and try to find the place in my book where I left off last night, while I listen to the silence outside. Then I hear the scrape of a snow shovel on my walkway. As I snuggle into the warmth of my cozy bed, I think of the difference in today and yesterday. Yes, I tell myself, there are advantages in being an older, retired person with no job to get to on a snowy morning such as this.

I recall those mornings of the past when I had been much younger and had worked at the University of Rhode Island. We had moved here from Santa Cruz, California, where we lived for 12 years and so I had forgotten how to drive or to live in the snow. I would dress in sweaters and coats until I could hardly perambulate, climb into my trusty little red VW, and pedal carefully down the road and up Kingston Hill making my white-knuckled way at about 10 miles per, praying aloud to the saints in Heaven to let me arrive safely at the office.

When I got there, I would often find I was the only one who had reported in that miserable snowy day. If I did not go in, however, I would likely find that I was the only one not there. That was a decision I did not have to make on this particular day and I feel all the happier for it as I open the latest Charles Todd book and settle in.

There had been other days when the sun was shining and birds were singing when I was retired and wished I still had a job to do because of loneliness or boredom. I tell myself and return to the adventures of Ian Rutledge.

######

RUTH AND POP

By Guida Cole Schmedinghoff

They didn't impress me at all when I answered the knock on the door on that quiet afternoon and found them standing there. They were an elderly couple and kind of all beige. He wore spectacles and khakis and a short-sleeved cotton shirt. She wore a simple cotton dress. They introduced themselves as Ruth and John McCullough. They had come to introduce themselves because they had taken the downstairs apartment in our building.

"Everybody calls me, Pop," was the first thing out of his mouth.

Ruth and Pop came to be almost family to us. Our two kids loved them; they seemed to enjoy the kids. When Pop told us he worked as an oiler at a local manufacturer, we could hardly believe it. He was so intelligent and knew so much about so many things. We would have guessed he would have a much more responsible job. Then Ruth confided that she had Multiple Sclerosis and, seeing how solicitous he was of her, we decided that was it. He had taken a non-demanding job so he could better care for her.

We moved into a home of our own but continued to see the two of them frequently. We noticed Ruth was getting more tired these days; she took long frequent naps during the afternoons. She was a chain smoker and one day her lit cigarette started a house fire while she was napping, causing Ruth's death by smoke inhalation.

Their son and daughter-in-law came to clean out their apartment and, in the course of helping sort things, I saw the newspaper clippings. Pop had mentioned he played the violin but had stopped when his fingers could no longer keep up with the music. He had not mentioned he was a well-known violinist, however. Indeed, he had played concerts across Europe as well as this country. We did think there might be a bit more to his playing when we noticed he always seemed a bit uncomfortable when he was at our house for dinner and we had some of our recordings playing. If our choice was traditional jazz and a little pop, perhaps and Pop would fidget and start a conversation. Finally, he confessed his own choice was classical. Still, he would listen politely and make admiring comments about the artist if he possible could, even about the guitar playing of Glenn Campbell who was hot that year.

And Ruth? According to another newspaper, she had been a welder during World War II when the shortage of men had caused women to go into the defense plants. The newspaper said she had won several awards for her skill as a welder in the airplane factory where she had worked, beating out most of the longtime male welders in competitions. Then one warm afternoon she fell from a ladder at work. At this point her disease was diagnosed and she was forced to resign.

We were thunderstruck. The thought of these two gentle, self-effacing people with colorful careers in their pasts was almost more than we could absorb. We had both assumed Ruth had spent her life being a homemaker and mother of their only child. Pop came over late one afternoon to bring me her cookbook. He said she had wanted me to have it. I still treasure it today though I must add that, as she herself always claimed, she was not much of a cook.

######

RANDOM ACTS OF KINDNESS

By Marie Younkin-Waldman

I think the concept of Random Acts of Kindness is great and whenever you do one you feel good. For example if you are standing in line at Dunkin Donuts you can pay for the person in front or in back of you no questions asked. Just say "Pay it forward". Doing little things that make people happy such as smiling at strangers when you are out and about is a good idea also unless you smile at someone who ends up following you home.

Once I bumped in to my husband recently at the hospital physicians building. "What are you doing here?" I said. "I just went down to your doctor's office to pick up your book and medicine that you had left there," he answered." I read about it on my smart phone and since I was in the area I decided to pick them up for you." That's an act of love.

This past year I had a "0" birthday. Several random acts of kindness occurred around that time. I ended up spending a month of celebrations for my birthday. My family went to dinner with grandchildren, children etc. at a fondue place. Friends in Florida took me to restaurants. Other friends still took me out when I returned from Florida. The birthday kept going on and on. Very kind.

I like to do things for people when they are not expecting it and watch them smile. I bought some pansies for the Sunday school children and then gave the leftover plants to various adults at coffee hour. When I have the money I like to send flowers to friends on special occasions or care packages to grandchildren at college. A few years ago my husband and I invited people at our church that had no place to go at Thanksgiving to come to our house.

When I was single and struggling as a private school teacher I needed a new car. When I mentioned it to my sister she said "How are you going to pay for it? I said "I'll take a loan." A couple of days later I got a check for $10,000 in the mail so I could buy a new car. That car gave me ten years of transportation back and forth to work enabling me to take care of my family.

When you open the paper every day and read about all the crime and ways people are hurting each other or swindling the system it is nice to know there is kindness in the world to keep you going and believing in the good. The little things do matter. How about opening the doors for older folks, letting someone have your place in line, giving someone some change at the store when they don't have enough or giving up your seat on a bus?

Last weekend my middle daughter (I have three daughters) came down and took my husband and me to brunch. Then she worked side by side with me in the garden weeding and spreading mulch and having fun. She knew she was going to be busy on Mother's Day so she made a time a week ahead to do something for me. It was a great surprise and a wonderful chance to have some one on one time with my busy daughter who shares the love of gardening.

A couple of weeks ago I had a close friend come over and made her a special lunch and waited on her. She has made me lunch many times and made me feel at home in her house. It was a chance to give her a break while she has been so busy lately caring for others. I received a beautiful little note from her saying how much it meant to her to be pampered and waited on while she has been so busy helping others in her family. I was glad to make her happy.

Life is a one time around thing so why not live it as pleasantly as possible? Life is really a gift that enables us many opportunities to do things for others as well as ourselves. It makes life so much more precious and enjoyable. So here's to random acts of kindness!!

8 May 2014

######

SILENCE CAN BE MORE THAN GOLDEN

By Marie Younkin-Waldman

When Linda gave us the assignment about silence my first thought was of a woman who said something to me many years ago. When this woman heard that I was unable to hear anything after my hearing aids were off she declared "But it must be so awful to be deaf!"

I wrote an article for The Providence Journal magazine in the eighties about this topic. (I can't seem to find the article at the moment.) I gave examples of the beauties of silence that I am able to experience. How do I experience them, let me count thy ways... I shall try to recall and perhaps add some more examples.

When I wake up in the morning all is quiet. I don't put my hearing aid and processor on right away. Instead I arise gently from my bed, walk slowly to the bathroom and then to the kitchen. I open the front door and feel the warm sunshine and see the brightness of the light as it plays through the branches of the trees in our front yard. I walk into my yard, unaware of the sounds of the children and their mothers walking down the street to the school bus. Instead I am mindful of the sights and feelings of the morning, the crisp air, the colors of the trees and the blue or gray sky. I pick up the newspaper and amble back into my house silently.

Breakfast between my husband and me is spent in silence as he, also has adopted this habit of not putting on his aid until after his shower. If he wants to ask me if I want oatmeal or eggs for breakfast he waves an oatmeal bowl in front of my face or an egg carton with a quizzical look on his face. We both eat our breakfast silently in front of the Today show and read the captions or we read the newspaper quietly. After our breakfast and showers we can talk to each other with our aids and processor on.

Let me see, silent baths are oh so comforting and calm as I stretch out under the bubbles in the warm water. Another tranquil experience takes place in the summer when I go to the Bay Campus beach nearby, take off my glasses and my hearing devices and go for a nice long swim in the cool water on a hot day. After returning to the beach I don't put my hearing devices on. I just towel off and lie down under the sun. It is the most relaxing feeling to just lie in the total silence on the sand under the warm sun while feeling the blood tingling refreshingly in my body after the cool swim.

At night Myron and I climb into bed after removing our hearing aids and my processor. If we have anything to say to each other we have to try our limited sign language which is more like a game of charades or we use the pencil and paper that I keep on the night table. (Except in the dark!) When the lights are out and it is pitch black it is not always total silence because that is when the ear wants to hear something when it can't and it creates noises of its own called "Tinnitus". That is unpredictable and sometimes intermittent. The silence in the dark is not always comfortable for me especially when Myron is away and I am alone. I can very easily imagine noises and sometimes wonder if someone is breaking into the house.

On the airplane when I don't want to hear the constant humming I remove my devices and relax with a book. It is the same when on a train or in the car. I usually tell Myron this if I am traveling with him unless I don't want him to know. Then the silence is even more golden!

November 18, 2013

######

THE FAVORITE ROOM

By Marie Younkin-Waldman

My favorite room in our house is a no brainer to those who know me. It is my sunroom. We put this addition on our house along with a great room about ten years ago. The sunroom is a room full of light that brings happiness to me any time of the year. It is my sanctuary.

The room faces West and South with windows on all three sides facing out and a "vanity" shaped window high under the ceiling to add character to the room. The walls are painted off white that appears light lemon yellow in the sunlight. Half of the room is arranged like a sitting room with a sofa, a couple of chairs and plants around. The African violets love it there and blossom like crazy. So do the large pots of geraniums that I bring inside over the winter and they bloom year round. The north end of the room has my desk, a small wooden filing cabinet and a book shelf. I only keep the papers and notebooks of the projects that I am currently working on in this room due to limited space and limited mind congestion. There are a couple of narrow shelves hung high on the walls. One has six teapots on it and the other has a multifarious collection of attractive artificial greenery, a painted birdhouse and a purple polka dotted watering can along with a stuffed bunny reclining against it like Peter Rabbit in McGregor's garden. The sign over the back glass door at the north end of my sunroom says" Bienvenue a Mon Jardin" and was a gift. The sign over the window frame on the south end of the room says "Live Well, Laugh Often, Love Much" and was another gift. The black and white wooden sign near my desk says "Think Outside The Box"and has a combination of four red glitter- sprinkled large wooden letters spelling" LOVE" resting on top of it. These were gifts to me. You get the picture.

This room represents me. There is a pink, yellow, green and white decorated collage that I made on a large poster board from recycled greeting cards and had laminated at Staples that is on one wall. It makes me smile as I see friends and loved ones represented there. Another wall has a large colored article from the Providence Journal, also laminated, with photos of and information about my daughter, the state trooper. Two other walls have pictures of serene scenes in Bermuda and a garden. This room is where I go at four o'clock in the afternoon to relax on the couch with a good book or a cup of tea. It is where I listen to the opera on the radio on Saturday afternoons with another cup of tea.

The sunroom is also my writing room. I have written two books in this room and many assignments for writing class, letters to the editor or thank you notes to friends and family at my desk. I love to look up from my computer when I am in the middle of writing a piece and see my garden outside the window. I feel surrounded by my garden which is another part of me. I hope my garden also reflects my creativity and tastes. I can watch the roses, lilacs, rose of Sharon bushes fully bloomed with hummingbirds flitting about them. I can see the goldfinch cradled on the birdfeeders in summer. I can see the little finches taking baths in my birdbath that has a small angel statue fountain in the center that my husband concocted for me. The fountain sound when my screen window is open is comforting.

Everyone needs their own special space to call their own. My sunroom is my special space. When the world is too much with us with its problems and challenges I retreat to my sunroom where I find peace, comfort and the ability to be myself.

1 October 2013

######

My Room At The Top Of The Stairs

By Doris Parisette

It is impossible not to be impressed by the glimmering sea and quivering ripples in the pond. It changes constantly. Every time I glance thru the glass doorway or look out a window I see something different. The wind, water, shadows, clouds keep changing. This is from my room in my turret—shaped lookout that sits up high from where I can view my world.

I can look south, west and north and watch. I really can't miss much for it surrounds me. I see the boats, kayaks, canoes and activity that attract everyone to the pond and watch the life on it. I look down the road and see what's going on. Lawns being cut, doggies walked, kids and adults on bikes. Families and visitors coming and going and the wildlife: turkeys strutting down the path to the edge of the pond, a fox, rabbits unending and the Birds: gulls, hawks, osprey, crows, songbirds so busy in the spring building their nests; seabirds swans, geese, taking off and landing, flocking on the lawn. Ducks ducking and bobbing, Herons standing in the pond and fishing; cormorants sitting on a rock drying their spread-out wings. I keep binoculars handy to zero them in close. Nature at my doorway.

The pond has a life of its own. Sometimes waves abound in the wind, foam whipping up on the shores; then there are the times it becomes like a mirror without a ripple just reflecting the sky and clouds. Schools of fish or hatching clam worms attract the seagulls and there is a ferocious feeding as they partake of the bounty and have a banquet.

This autumn I saw thousands of bank swallows swarming and diving back and forth around my turret and flying across the pond chasing insects. One time they lined up on the electric wire flocking in an unending row.

Each season brings a different look. Now in the autumn the colors are again changing around the pond, the sun's rays are at a different slant, the shadows are lengthening; birds and Monarch butterflies are migrating. At times the days are sharp and clear, on others the sea mist rolls in and envelops my little tower. Constantly different, always fascinating.

The sunsets are glorious. A never ending display often enough to take your breath away with their beauty.

Each season has its own signature. The winters with the snow on the frozen pond looks like a tundra. The big flakes swirling around outside my room are beautiful.

I am warm and secure in my room with its pictures, paneling, futon, computer desk from which I can see everything and can watch the ever-moving scenery on the tip of the peninsula. I thank my lucky stars for this promise of forever.

Heaven can wait; this is paradise.

October 3, 2013

######

NEW ENGLAND SEASONS

By Doris Parisette

There is one thing about New England weather; it is always changing.

Friends who have retired elsewhere, though it may be warmer and easier on the "ole bod," miss our seasons. No wonder so many people make a pilgrimage in the fall to view the scenery and glorious colors and vacation here in the summer, ski in the winter. I like the changes of season and the contrast. Each has its own special allure and makes the others more interesting. Each defines a refreshing non-sameness. Each one leads into something else. Nature's own moving time clock.

ALL SEASONS

I love it here in springtime, the summertime and fall.
I love our changing seasons, the difference of them all.
The sunlit days, the moon bright nights, the winter snow or squall
I relish each and every one
I'm a Yankee after all

A spring that reawakens, when buds push up the earth
The birds return and sing their song for nesting, laying, birth.
Of sun splashed sprays of shining waves, the summer blooms of
worth
Bless the months of summertime
with friends and fun and mirth.

Then autumn sends its message with shorter, crisper days
With harvests ripe and darkened nights, lengthened sunshine rays.
That vibrant height of color throughout New England sends
the glory and the beauty in a final painted blaze.

Now winter blows its snowy breath, it freezes all around
It's icy blast and flurries blanketing the ground
Sometimes with such a silence, not a thing to hear
The cold, sharp, quiet clearness, that doesn't make a sound.

As the seasons vary, with each a different kind
Create the moods and images to flow across your mind
If you do not like it, be patient, wait awhile
There's another day, another time coming right behind.

######

MY FAVORITE ROOM IN MY HOUSE

By Alice Rose-Mott Huggins

My favorite room in my house is the cellar. It wasn't always. It used to be spooky. I dreaded going there. It smelled of mildew, leaks and floods following rainstorms. I feared rodents seeking a warm winter home.

When my husband died, I was left to handle the dreaded cellar jobs on my own— checking the oil, adjusting the water temperature, doing laundry. I pondered over what might be done to conquer my fears. Fortunately, a young neighbor, Mary Beth Hobe, was looking for work. Maybe, together, we could transform the cellar into a real room. The thought excited us. We began work.

We filled cracks in the stone foundation. We painted the walls with several coats of sealer. The cement over dirt floor, which had been painted battleship grey, became sea green. We wallpapered between the ceiling beams with Matisse gift-wrap purchased at Rhode Island School of Design gift shop. Walls took on a brighter hue thanks to Benjamin Moore's China White.

How to decorate? Another thought entered our heads: a lifetime collection of artwork and photographs was in albums that were rarely opened. More were in cardboard boxes stored in the attic. Why not display them on the China White walls?

Now, when friends come to visit, they seldom leave without saying, *would you mind if we take another look in your cellar?* Often, they will find shots of themselves. Sometimes, they will catch glimpses of mutual friends who no longer walk the earth. Then, we'll reminisce about past times shared with the deceased.

Young parents often discover photos of themselves as young children playing on the beach, fishing in a pond or playing croquet.

Recently, the cellar stairs were painted Marine Blue. A carpet runner was faux painted in the center of the stairs. A faux carpet at the base of the stairs copied the runner design. Now I enjoy going into the previously dreaded cellar. On days when the wind blows and the ferry doesn't run and airplanes are grounded, one could easily become depressed. That's when I step down into my favorite room rejoicing in the memories on the China White walls.

######

PHOBIA
By Alice Rose-Mott Huggins

I see what I think is a dead mouse on my cellar floor. It turns out to be a leaf, shaped like a dead mouse.

I'm reading a book. As I turn the page, there is an illustration of a rodent. I either cover it with a blank piece of paper or skip to the next page.

Medical programs on TV often include experimental research photos of white rats. Quickly, I reach for the off button.

One of my daughters has this same problem with spiders — another, with frogs. Is this inherited? Is it a feminine phenomenon? My sons do not suffer these anxieties.

Recent studies claim that rodents behave much like humans. They sympathize with their kind. If a rat is caught in a trap, its friend will hover around the trap seemingly trying to release it. When there is no hope, it appears to mourn its loss.

As severe as my phobia is, I once had a strange experience. It was late April. We were opening our Block Island house. When I went to inspect our upstairs guest room there was a dead rat on one of the twin beds. Strangely, I wasn't spooked.

I believe that, in nature, everything is interrelated. We are all part of the whole. However, April's opening the house experience did not cure my rodent phobia.

Should the unexpected scratching of an unexpected mouse wake me in the night, I'd probably dress in a hurry and check in to the nearest Holiday Inn.

A snake and his relative lived in my fireplace living room woodpile for weeks before finding their way out. How did they get in? How did they get out? The spooked visitors but, strangely, did not spook me. We lived together in harmony.

Not so with rodents.

######

REUNION

By Alice Rose-Mott Huggins

On Monday morning, March 12, 2012, I had the privilege of attending Betty Cotter's mother's funeral service. Betty's eulogy, straight from her heart, rang many bells that were similar to my own New England Yankee background.

For me, the service turned out to be a REUNION with my deceased ancestors.

The Baptist minister, who led Betty's service, brought my father's funeral back into my mind. His open casket was displayed in the Bellevue's front parlor where we lived on Block Island. Reverend Calder Miller, the West Side Baptist minister, read from Ecclesiastes. Friends and neighbors sang, "I Come to the Garden Alone, while the dew is still on the roses," "The Old Rugged Cross" and "Amazing Grace."

We recited the 23rd Psalm, which everyone knew by heart. Our neighbor, Cornelius Rose and his two sons, Neil and Redge, were among the pallbearers. The casket rolled toward the Block Island cemetery where my father's remains were lowered next to his parents.

Betty Cotter's mother taught in a one-room schoolhouse, complete with a wood stove and chilly outhouse. My father's sister, my Aunt Gertrude, taught grades one through eight at Block Island's one-room Neck School. Neck School's foundation still remains on my inherited island property.

Primary years found me at the Harbor School. It's now the location of the Island's town hall. Wood stoves and chilly outhouses were still part of the package when I entered first grade.

I was often in trouble in Grade 3. I couldn't catch on to the Palmer Method. Ink spilled on my desk and stained my hands.

Betty spoke of the Depression. Her memories were similar to mine. Our families were on the lower end of the income bracket; but we were not unhappy. We raised our own food in a sparsely populated Rhode Island setting. We drank raw milk poured into glass bottles where heavy cream exploded to the top. Sometimes, my father would skim the cream and churn it into butter in the Homestead's milk room.

Betty's eulogy sparked in me, an unexpected REUNION with my own deceased family.

######

How Do You Like That?!

Cindy Arrighi

Here I am at my daughter's basketball game. She's the point guard. So is her teammate. Jackson is a Junior. Action Jackson, they call her. Of course for more than one reason! It's the fourth quarter with a score of 44 to 42 Toll Gate! The heat is on! Jacksons got the ball at half court with three seconds left to the game! She shoots! The crowd is silent! She misses! My heart races! I hear myself blurt out a huge sigh. Ugh—Jackson's mother, sitting alone three rows in front of me hears it!

She turns and yells at me in her gruff, argumentative tone, "You think that's funny?"

I'm shocked! I didn't think I had laughed.

But she asks again, more pronounced now, "You think that's funny?"

I ignored her, as I didn't quite know how to react to such craziness!

If you know anything about competitive sports you know how crazy parents can behave. I had been trying to ignore her, but I was feeling the loss of the game too. So I slinked my way down to her bleacher seat, sat right next to her, and said with vengeance, "What's your problem? No. I didn't think it was funny!"

She said nothing, but got up and started to walk toward the court. I followed her. She searched the crowd, looking for her daughter.

I was thinking *this is ridiculous. We're on the same team!* I began to feel perhaps she was intimidated. My freshman daughter made the varsity basketball team and her daughter was a junior on the varsity team! I get it now. How will her daughter shine with a freshman outdoing her? But aren't parents adults?

She ignored me and this was making me angry.

I was proud of my daughter for making the varsity team and had hoped Jackson could be a good mentor for her. Apparently she didn't know what that meant. The competition and jealousy showed in all kinds of ways.

I moved up and stood next to her on the court, shoulder to shoulder. "Come on," I said, "are you kidding me? We are adults aren't we?"

She said nothing.

About then, my daughter found me. "Mom come on let's get out of here."

I looked at Jacksons Mom and said, "Geez, I thought your daughter would be bigger than she is and be glad for the opportunity to mentor a good player. Now I know why she can't!"

I walked away.

To this day, I wonder if she ever recalls that time. But I will never forget how I felt. I quickly realized Jackson was an arrogant young woman who would probably end up in a D ranked college. (She did, and with a false sense of who she was.) I felt disappointed for my daughter who had to look forward to being in competition with a young woman on her own team, though not on her side. To be in a constant state of defeat and uncertainty with a teammate still doesn't make sense to me. It's a lose-lose for both girls.

As a parent, all I could do was coach my daughter to be the best she could be as a teammate and player. My daughter didn't become a basketball star, but she still plays pick-up games in the South End of Boston with whoever's on the court—men and women! She's still the best little 5'2" point guard with the best reverse lay up's I've ever seen, Yup, I'm on her team!

######

STARTING OVER AGAIN!
By Cindy Arrighi

Although I really have no clue
Beginning again I have done before
Clearly I know it's nothing new
Dumping the past can make you feel blue

Easy street has always been my path.
Focus on the future?
Give me a break! I'd rather take a bath!
Happy as a clam for sure!

Instantly life demands I change my scene
Jiffy pop, spinning like a top
Key West is cool beans!
Longing for life in my flip flops!

Moving on down the road
Name me a tune I can sing
Optimistically I'll sing it over and over again!
Perpetually I'm dreaming of something

Quickly quitting just ain't my thang!
Ridiculous thoughts run through my head.
Swirling and twirling, dang!
Tripping over thoughts of dread

Unexpected moments hoping for sterling
Victory has been mine
Waves of doubt still often peeking
Xylophones twanging sweet tunes in time

Yummy fruity thoughts remind me of tweaking
Zig zagging through life on a dime!

9 June 2014

######

THE CASE OF THE MISSING SCRIVENERS

By Linda Langlois

By all accounts, I should be in Sing-Sing,
atoning for a life of petty crime,
I might well have been a lyin' two-bit hustler...
Raincoat's runner or Rumpy's sidekick or like the time
I helped that dame, Gladys, dump the guzzler in the drink.
A woman stood between me and that underbelly life,
a pipe-smokin'...cigar-totin'...tobacco-lovin' woman
saved me from a life of strife.
"My name's Racy ... Rick Racy... I'm a cop."

o o o o o o o o

"Ohhhhh, son...the truth shall set ye free ... a cop...?"
This from Solomon, Rick's partner, friend and nemesis.
Sol marvels how life with Rick is wrought with chance,
with risk and a long way from Spud Island
and the prison life they don't miss.

Rick's sojourn as undercover inmate had been drawing to a close
while Solomon's life as prison chaplain posed questions in his
soul. They'd met in writers' group, a weekly meet of words,
writings designed to stretch the mind, foster creations
on the verge of imagination.

Rick wrote of gritty streets and boyhood pranks
while Solomon's island images overlaid his wartime angst.
Lately Sol was remembering the army's trek across the sea,
the crazy zig-zag to hide from U-boats,
the enemy beneath an ocean as dark and scary as the night.
The young island lad away from home found it hard to write
about the war.

When Rick left prison driving south, along went Sol to this
sleepy coastal New England town where no one wondered why
an ex-chaplain and ex-cop would set up shop as private eyes.

"I was a cop, till that dame, Gladys, did me in...
                    lost more than my badge."

o o o o o o o o

Above the entrance, a bell jangles and a woman walks
              through the door...a Bogart kind of woman:
long-leggity, ageless, secrets in her eyes, smoky-shaded glasses.
She glides across the room, heels clicking the floor,
           thin, red heels, her skirt brushing...
She removes a leather glove, extends her hand to Rick—
           no polish, no rings - a smooth cool hand.

Her voice is husky and low:
           "Mychaela—Angelina Sorentino," she says,
           "my friends call me Mykey."

"Sooooooo, ok, is it ... Mikey then," I ask.

           "We'll see."
She shrugs off her white Burberry coat...tucks a blonde curl
behind her ear, a diamond-studded ear, sits in a waiting chair.

"Suppose you tell us why you're here," Sol says, watching Rick.
The woman takes a Newport menthol from her Gucci purse,
           taps the end against a silver case.

I nod to the No Smoking sign Sol has hung on the wall.

"Oh, I don't smoke," she claims...
           she's reporting missing persons, though
           she can't recall their real names.

"We meet on Wednesday nights...down by the lake.
"Shadow Lake," she adds, like we wouldn't know.

"Who's we," asks Sol

"**We** are writers. You can't just go; you need to be invited."

But she won't say, by whom.

I remember my buddy down at the precinct, Lieutenant Winnetou, talking about a secret society or something ... led by some mad-cap professor; oh, what's his name - something weathery. Rain, that's it. Yeah...Professor Rain.

Her info's sketchy, to say the least. Sol takes notes as I piece together her words. The missing guy's called Cedric and the woman's....Paulala. I swear that's how she says it...Paulala.

"That Wednesday was a blue moon; that's why we were there.
Soon Cedric starts to read and the wind rose."
Her voice is whispery, soft, kinda creepy, weaving a tale of
creatures shifting from human to not and back again.
She says this is how Cedric writes, like from an alternate world.

From the corner of my eye, I see Sol lift a brow as she continues:

"I remember how dark was that night but for a weird corridor of
light, from the middle of the lake to the shore, like the moon was
beckoning us."

*She suddenly stops, looks around at me, at Sol, not really seeing us.
Know what I mean? Like she's in a dream. Then...*

"They weren't there," she says.

"Whoa, who's weren't where," Sol asks. She ignores him, says, "And they're not here. They aren't – anywhere. "I need to report them, missing."

I lean across the desk. "That was in August," I say.
I'd seen it on the news, had never heard of it before....Blue Moon. What the hell was that all about? Some sorta folklore, I guessed.

"That's right," she says, "the twenty-first."

"It's November"! I point to the window at the snow.
"Has no one thought to phone the police"?

*She's indignant. **She's** indignant!*

"Police think they're a couple, ran away. Police won't listen when we say they're not a couple; they're missing. "

"So, what's Rain have to say," I ask.

She stands abruptly, "I have to go." And out she goes.

o o o o o o o o

My buddy at the precinct, Lieutenant Winnetou, takes my call.

"Win, how goes it, man; you doin' ok," I ask.

"Ya, Ya, fine, I'm fine. What can I do for you"?

"That mad-cap professor, lives down by the lake? ... from the university...Rain? He poppin' up on your radar anywhere"?

"Why"? *Win's nothing if not circumspect.*

"Well, I heard he runs some sorta group thing, like in the '60s? ...book people, you know.   Apparently, two of 'em have turned

up, missing. Heh! Heh! I love that phrase: turned up missing.
Kinda like waking up, dead."

"Uh Rick, watcha got? Kind of busy here."

"Oh, sorry. So two months ago…that's the other thing. This
happened last August, night of the Blue Moon (you ever hear of
one of those)? Anyway, so there's a "reading"… I don't know …
incantation? Spell? Voodoo? More likely, some sort of weedy-
thing going on, if you ask me. Anyway, when the smoke (so to
speak) cleared, this buddy and his girl or a girl, are gone. Poof!
Vanished into thin air."

Lieutenant Winnetou looks at the phone in his hand: *Two
months ago? And we're just hearing about this now?*

"So, maybe you could meander down there? Take a look around?
Pay Prof Mad-Cap, a call"?

"Meander? You should be a writer, Rick. I'll see what I can do."

o o o o o o o o

The second Guinness slides down smoother than the first and
Win knows it's time to leave. Hunched inside his bomber jacket,
elbows on the bar, he breathes in, remembering … her laughter
at cracks in the faded leather of his sleeves.

She bought him a new jacket once that he's never worn.
They both laughed at that. He's so tired of her being gone.

When the band strikes up "Danny Boy" Win is out the door.
Turning left on Main, he heads for the lake. He's looking forward
to his transfer, a new life, a new state. He can't wait to return to
research, maybe canoe again.

The woods above the lake are dark and Win's glad for the clouds.
As he picks his way among the trees, he is unprepared for the
onslaught of memories: walking East to West.
The best night? Saturday. Soldiers loud with drink on the path.

The boy thinking one last kilometer to the border, then rest.

As if summoned, the moon rises, exposed above the trees.

○ ○ ○ ○ ○ ○ ○ ○

From a window overlooking the lake, Professor Rain watches the woods, intrigued by movement among the trees. Rain thinks of himself as Lord of the Manor, overseer of all he sees. He runs his thumb down the strap of red suspenders he wears for effect, ponders his next step. He picks up the cell phone lying by his keys.

○ ○ ○ ○ ○ ○ ○ ○

From the kitchen, Mrs. Professor Rain strains to listen, willing the refrigerator hum to cease. Rain's decision to sell their condo, move across the hall perplexes her still, fills her with unease. Though they now live lake-side and it's lovely, he's only interested in the view, after dark. And really, she thinks, what is there to see. They've been years together, she loved their retired life ... till he grew distant, taciturn. He only wants to write.

Her years connected with the town make her visible, a public figure so to speak ... which has her wondering what folks are saying. Should she sneak out at night, creep down to the lake? She isn't one to balk at fate but she grows weary of worrying.

○ ○ ○ ○ ○ ○ ○ ○

Special Agent Stefan adjusts his telescope, aligns the lens inside the russet curtain of his rented condo. For three months since that weird August moon, there was nothing. And now, a blood moon plays peek-a-boo with clouds, tree limbs lean into the wind like skeletons against the sky.
Stefan's not a superstitious man but his antenna is on high.

He knows Rain's watching from the floor below, knows Rain's in tune. Whatever looms out there in the night, Stefan's sure Rain knows. Early on, he befriended Rain, joined the town's writing group but couldn't get himself invited inside Rain's inner loop.

In the distance, Stefan spots a firefly, just one, odd so late in the season. He doesn't *see* what he's seeing, doesn't "get" the reason for the cyclic light.

○ ○ ○ ○ ○ ○ ○ ○

Two more puffs and she'll go up. She knows Captain Deck doesn't like the smoke, but she needs to relax, re-orient herself. She doesn't want to mess up this opportunity. She's been on the run for such a long time and this isn't the craziest work she's ever done.
Standing at the rail when the ferry moves through the night, she's taken the deepest breaths she's had in years.
She loves being in the dark, alone. She lets go, the old fears.

She likes working with the Captain...he's quiet, kind...not much of a talker. She doesn't mind. Most nights, he sits up top, his beach chair tilted, his feet on the railing. Strumming a string bass guitar, he hums, softly.
She's used to rock 'n roll, folk, words that move through sound. The Captain's music has no words; you think your own and that process calms her down.

○ ○ ○ ○ ○ ○ ○ ○

Deck looks out where Loch Isle lies across the lake, strumming his bass, listening for footfalls in the woods, in case the three have trouble finding their way.
Deck takes his time, his mind wandering, fingering scales, playing notes, composing a piece for the gathering.

Funny he should end up here in this quirky little town.
From the farm to the army to the insane; hmmm... maybe all connected on some cosmic ground. He ferries folks, that's what he does, while playing music in his head. Though his intent was to escape, a separate peace he found instead.

Deck watches the moon, decides to tidy the room below for May.
He knows she won't relax till daylight, till the moon is down.
Remnants linger for her of war, danger when the moon is full
and white and round.

First ferry leaves at dawn. For some reason it takes a long time to reach Loch Isle. Deck doesn't know exactly how far away it is. He doesn't ferry very often; there's no schedule. Folks come round from away when they want a ride. As a rule, locals never go to the isle, unless they've something to hide.

∘ ∘ ∘ ∘ ∘ ∘ ∘ ∘

Ma-ri-a leans on the rail in peace, wind blowing back her hair. She's excited about this day. She's never been to Loch Isle. She lives on her own island, suits her just fine. Lines from the sunrise edge the sky and she smiles into the air.

At this point in a long road of bumps and sharp curves, she leans on a rail in peace, wind blowing back her hair. Like the war - one hell of a sharp curve there...turned her left when she'd been heading in the right direction. She still thinks about the soldier on that road.

She was always *that girl in the wind*, aptly named...playing golf, cutting grass, calling forth Miss Kitty.
Even now, she wants the summer free.

∘ ∘ ∘ ∘ ∘ ∘ ∘ ∘

All day Sally waits for May's call. *She's such a gadabout*, thinks Sally, knowing May would never be outside in the moonlight.
So, where is she?
Sally had a *Heidi* look, growing up. Folks say she's lived an ordinary life. Has she? Maybe then...when living near the "rich people's beach" meant summer jobs, tips.
A gentle Grandpa and a late curfew meant hanging out with Jean and the others on a dock in a town blacked-out by the reach of war. Singing.

Rationing was real, nights scary with the squeal of air raid drills. Boys were scarce, money more so. But through it all,
they swam together at Watch Hill.

Now, when sleep eludes, she moves her mind to somehow land
on that same beach *with the sun shining down and the soft
whispered sound of waves splashing on the sand.*

o o o o o o o o

May's daughter drives her down to the lake, walks with her
through the woods, all the while watching the waxing luna
overhead.
May's life now is one of lunches and laughing with her friends.
                "And why not," she's often said.

May reads her New York Times, finds articles that lend
themselves to comment, surrounded by painted walls of her
beloved's art.
She rides the train into Manhattan, visits her old haunts.
May lives in Wakefield now, but New York City has her heart.

o o o o o o o o

Daybreak!
Rose stands in the shadow of Loch Isle's lighthouse, watching the
strobe streak the beach a hundred wooden steps below. She sees
Pierre running with his pups. They're older now than he is.
    She knows he won't hear her if she calls. She waves; he waves
    too. His eyes look to the turret, to the woman from watching
                        within its walls.

o o o o o o o o

Helen, the "Lighthouse Lady" as she's known on the island has
run the lighthouse twenty years since Frank's death. Near the
end, the island council asked her to take over as lighthouse *Keep.*
                And Helen had said yes.
She knows when the island mows its grass, walks its dogs, sees
secrets she'll never tell. She loves the wind and the shadows and
the sea gulls, and the sunlight till it blotted out the tower stair,
                    and Helen fell.

○ ○ ○ ○ ○ ○ ○ ○

And so, Pierre came home from Paris, left his art, left the wine,
gentle nights upon the Seine, left his heart with Gigi,
moved in with Helen to help her mend.

He loves to tell the story of the morning in the cove. Walking
Eastward with his pups, still in slippers, still in robe when
swoosh, a fleeting white from a corner of his eye.
Not a gull, not a ghost but *something* on the fly.

Later, from the lighthouse window Pierre finds his proof:
sees a Great Snowy Owl on Jerry's cottage roof,

Her talons hug its edge while he wonders where she's from.
She watches him with yellow eyes, looks north, looks west,
white against the rising of the sun.

○ ○ ○ ○ ○ ○ ○ ○

Rose looks out to America...as islanders call the mainland,
thrilled she followed Bill's suggestion to turn the
Homestead into an inn.
Her ancestors would not approve of strangers moving through
the halls of Uncle Edward's farm. But for Rose, it's a perfect
blend: one-time strangers - now new friends, adventures, stories
unending. New people, new places, new pleasures sought,
Rose circles the globe without leaving her porch.

Oh, she's late, daydreaming again, with all she has to do.
Rose has two new guests...more folks coming. Still, she lingers
above the beach, her thoughts wandering; while out on the reach,
the ferry's horn is sounding.

○ ○ ○ ○ ○ ○ ○ ○

The girls came on the weekend, so young and yet, so talented –
Rhode Island's own Co-Poets, Laureate. On sabbatical from life,
as lived in the "real" world, from love, as lived in fantasy.
They soak up the island, its vibes, its mystique ... its energy.

Rose marvels at their *Laissez Faire,* they walk the beach, not
always together, search for shells, sea glass, whatever, always
with a notebook, always mindless of the weather...

Juniper Luna and Aurora, published poets of truth and fate,
      of passionate lies and wild rides and chance encounters
      of promises made – promises taken too lightly.
When the girls called Rose about visiting the island,
      she warned them: not a word was to be spoken
            about the gathering.

Hurry along, Rose, she picks up the basket at her feet,
      her coffee cooling, unwraps the newspaper on the way
      to the dock, stops cold, exclaims, *"Oh, what the Hell"*
      reading the headline with shock:

Loch Isle Times: Frances McCartney comes to Loch Isle

Ms. McCartney, a Rhode Island historian became an international
legend with her *"Eighties Ladies"*... historical fiction, the tabloids
called it. Originally thought to be of little interest to the general
public, the book went viral, as they say nowadays...*caught on
fire*...stayed five weeks on The New York Times' Bestseller List.
Book stores could not keep the book in stock. Libraries had
months-long Reserve Lists. Rumor has it, Steven Spielberg is
considering Dame Judi Dench, Angela Lansbury, or Maggie Smith.

Sepia photographs of young beautiful women, resemblances
across families not related, causing pause among readers...and
certain family members. Intrigue, fashion, Hollywood—family
stories told against a backdrop of war, the Depression, stock
market crash, international travel and, of course, the Titantic.

The true identity of the 80's Ladies was guarded, adding fuel to
the rumors, juice to the stories.
When interviewed, Ms. McCartney deflects the query, ignores the
question, smiles demurely.

○ ○ ○ ○ ○ ○ ○ ○

Rose sits abruptly on a stone wall along the road. Oh, those girls, guests of honor are always a secret. It's her promise of peace and quiet, an invisible stay to the rich and famous who find their way to her inn as guests, unbothered by islanders, who couldn't care less who they are.

She saw Aurora and Juniper Luna last night on the pier with other young folks; she had no idea the reporter was there among them. Well...Rose has secrets of her own: she **is** an 80's Lady.

As is Helen of lighthouse fame and Celia, Loch Isle's own mayor, whose name became legend when she reversed the ferry, sent it back to America. Drunken kids roared, parents applauded when she shut down the bar on board.

Of Midwestern stock, Celia was a formidable woman, a classic beauty from *the day.* She'd lived all over, including Turkey and for years was an agent with the CIA.

No one messes with Celia.

○ ○ ○ ○ ○ ○ ○ ○

Kelsey glances at the clock, relaxes when she hears the ferry's engine blast. Since early dawn, foghorns had been sounding off the coast, which meant the walk downhill from the Inn could be slippery, like glass.

She pulls croissants from the oven, wraps them warm
in hand-stitched towels, embroidered in blues and greens of the ocean and the grass: *Mary's Teahouse of a September Sun.*
She'd suggested to Mary, they should meet the boat, bring bakery baskets, sell warm welcomes to the folks, disembarking.

Kelsey pulls her sweater close, sets out for the dock.
Her writer friend works the ferry and they'd concocted
a hot idea: one novel from two points of view.

Each author writes her character in, the scene already chosen.
Then the authors meet, smooth the edges of a novel taking shape
beyond their wildest expectations.

o o o o o o o o

Mary turns from the window, surveys the teahouse of her
dreams, remembers her mother, whose gene for gentility was
bequeathed, birthing Mary's idea: create a sanctuary of serenity,
a relaxing retreat.

Mary notes her lone customer - same as every morn. Beryl
Bronson scribbles in her notebook, her face drawn, worn down
by guilt?
Beryl has no friends, speaks to no one, stink-eyes her neighbors.
She roams the island: sputtering, muttering *Agnes*.
A love affair gone wrong, the interloper's demise, long laid at
Beryl's door. Some say a guilty conscience drove her mad,
but no one knows for sure.
Mary's too kind to turn her away, finds her sad, lets her stay.

o o o o o o o o

Sandy crosses the street to the teahouse,
        feels a chill in November's air.
She needs to think in silence, drink soothing tea,
        write away her cares.

o o o o o o o o

Meanwhile, back in America:

Lieutenant Winnetou moves to Maine, resumes his membrane
research, walks the howling winter woods, sometimes alone,
sometimes not.

Professor and Mrs. Rain move to North Carolina, to see what
there is to see.

Special Agent Stefan sails into the sunset, humming "my life, my love and my lady is the sea."[1]

Mykey wins an AMTRAK fellowship, rides the rails, wins a Pulitzer with her memoir: "Murder on the Acela Express."

Rick and Sol excel as private eyes. In this sleepy, coastal New England town lie many secrets and secrets pay the rent.

And Cedric and Paulala? Yes indeedy, a couple—who knew?

######

1 "Brandi" by The Looking Glass, 1972